5
things

KATHY B. NELSON

things

What every guy should do and every girl
should wait on before getting married.

TATE PUBLISHING
AND ENTERPRISES, LLC

Published by Tate Publishing & Enterprises, LLC
127 E. Trade Center Terrace | Mustang, Oklahoma 73064 USA
1.888.361.9473 | www.tatepublishing.com

Tate Publishing is committed to excellence in the publishing industry. The company reflects the philosophy established by the founders, based on Psalm 68:11,
"The Lord gave the word and great was the company of those who published it."

Book design copyright © 2014 by Tate Publishing, LLC. All rights reserved.
Cover design by Jim Villaflores
Interior design by Mary Jean Archival

Published in the United States of America

ISBN: 978-1-63306-024-1
Family & Relationships / Love & Romance
14.08.27

Dedication

To my husband Rick, who has shown me all of the disciplines talked about in this book. After 32 years you are still the man I would want to marry.

To my daughters Katie and husband Jay & Lisa and husband Jonathan, for being personal cheerleaders on this journey with me, always encouraging. Thank you for loving Jesus. Thank you for giving us Jude and Georgia.

To Mom, for being a faithful example of how teaching God's word never gets old or boring, no matter what age you are teaching.

To Daddy, who is in his heavenly home now, for leaving a legacy of humor and a contagious love for all people. Those gifts have made my life so fun.

To all of my family for helping me believe I could actually do this and not to be afraid.

To youth, single adults and collegiate students I have met over the years, especially from Louisiana Tech University. You inspired the contents of this book and I will forever be grateful for your part in my life.

Acknowledgements

For the word of God is quick, and powerful, and sharper than any twoedged sword, piercing even to the dividing asunder of soul and spirit, and of the joints and marrow, and is a discerner of the thoughts and intents of the heart.

Hebrews 4:12 (KJV)

Katie Garcia, Lisa Stapp, Melissa Sullivan, Sandy Allen and Helene Shaw – for the time spent helping me put the words I have spoken into words on a page. Your insights and academic excellence have been priceless.

Rosalyn Fluty – for sharing your gift of art and photography in order make a more beautiful book.

Contents

Preface 11

Count the Cost 17

The Myths We Are Told 23

What about Boaz? 31

The Fundamentals 35

Thing No. 1 Favor 43

Thing No. 2 Provision 57

Thing No. 3 Protection 67

Thing No. 4 Affirmation 79

Thing No. 5 Integrity 89

Redeemed 99

FAQ's 105

Preface

Twenty years ago at a marriage conference, I failed. A local church hosted a marriage conference featuring a recently written book by a psychologist that detailed the perceived needs of husbands and wives based on surveys and discussions with some of his clients over the years. The group attending consisted of churchgoing couples at various stages of marriage. A few single adults attended as well, hoping to glean helpful information. Random laughter and rolling of the eyes could be heard and seen all over the room as each item of need was listed. According to the author's research, the top five needs husbands listed were to fulfill him sexually, to participate with him in his recreational interests, to keep herself looking attractive, to take care of the household needs, and to respect him. We were each given a checklist in order to determine our success in meeting our spouse's needs.

I'm sure there were some women who scored 100 percent and felt like they were the poster-wife of a godly woman. But after that brief, lighthearted moment came the feeling of discouragement. I saw heads drop and eyes fixed on the floor. I could tell I was not the only one who fell short of meeting the proposed "standards," and a feeling of failure set in. The voices in my head were warring over whether or not I would listen and yield to the lies Satan was whispering in my ear at that very moment.

These perceived needs of men made sense in light of our culture of selfishness, media influence and focus we have on body image. However, I felt my mental red flags go up and these needs caused me to wrestle in my spirit. I did not really understand why at that time, but I do remember feeling like such a loser. I remember wondering if my husband was disappointed in me. It was a terrible emotional place to find myself.

Before our speaker could move forward with further discussion, my friend, who is single and had never been married, was bold enough to raise her hand and break the awkward silence of the room. She confessed her singleness might prevent her from knowing a whole lot about marriage issues, but after listening to these lists of perceived needs and particularly the men's list of needs, she felt compelled to ask, "I am just wondering if any of you Christian men in here are embarrassed by this list that represents your top five needs? These needs seem so worldly and temporary and basically shallow. Are you all okay with this?"

Awkward silence.

My spirit continued to wrestle throughout the rest of the session. When we finally made our exit to the car, I burst into tears confessing to my husband that I felt like he really had a loser wife. In his kind and gentle way he reminded me how much he loved me. He affirmed areas in my life that were important to him and assured me I was all he needed and wanted. But, I still could not reconcile what it was that had my heart at such unrest during that conference session.

As years went by I continued to read about and hear more teaching concepts about how single adults should treat each other, know about each other, and handle their dating relationship. Then there were all of the clever suggestions for behaviors and tips for keeping happy marriages. Most of these principles and suggestions that were directed to Christian men and women could have been taken out of any secular men's magazine. There did not seem to be many distinctions between men who were followers of Christ and men who weren't regarding what is important in Christian dating and marriage. *Seriously*, shouldn't there be a difference?

Then it came to me. The feeling of failure came as a result of women being judged and measured by the opinions and preferences of men in our culture and not by the standards set out for us in Scripture. Scriptural standards are the highest standards we can attain. My life often falls short of those standards with God's standards come the resources of the

Holy Spirit which enables us to live out those principles and precepts God has required of us.

According to Covenant Eyes, an Internet accountability and filtering service, statistics show that 68% of young men and 18% of young women say they are addicted to pornography. And from my experience listening to young adults over the years I believe these numbers could easily be much higher.

During a recent gathering of primarily churched college students, they were asked to write down the areas of sin they struggle with most. A good 93% of these students, both guys and girls, were viewing pornography at least once a week and listed it as their primary struggle. If these percentages reflect the issues on the minds of guys and girls in the church, would it not make sense that surveying them regarding what they feel their needs are might reveal a clouded and perverted perspective to their answers? If their minds have been saturated with so many pornographic images and videos, why are we surprised when their needs reflect such shallow, self-serving desires?

Of course, it is good to share with your loved one honestly and clearly what your needs are. But, somewhere we bought into the lie that *our* perceived needs in relationships and marriages are more valuable and important than meeting the needs of the one we love. Here is what the Scriptures teach we actually need from each other as well as what we need to be to each other: "Do nothing from selfishness or empty conceit, but with humility of mind regard one another as more important than yourselves" Philippians 2:3 (NASB)

What I was hearing at each of these events began to become clear. While this information was interesting, informative, and even offered some great tools to consider as help in your relationships, they came up short on what God's Word trains us to seek. I was measured and judged as a wife by the opinions and preferences from a survey of men and not by the principles established by God's Word. I determined in my heart right then that I would not be a wife who is tossed to and fro by the whims of every thought and opinion that is taught regarding what I should be and what I should do in my marriage. My success as a wife—or just as a woman of God—will *only* be measured by the plumb line of the infallible, life-giving Word of God. God's standards are the highest we should ascribe to, and though they require sacrifice, discipline, and dying to one's self, God's plan comes with the resources of all of heaven and the power of his Holy Spirit. Almighty God can enable me to make the changes I need to make and begin obeying what he has required of me as a wife.

It's like choosing to drink from the well that will run dry or drinking from the living water that will never leave you thirsty. It's like choosing to eat bread that fills your stomach or eating from the bread of life that will never leave you hungry. When I chose to abandon these secular suggestions, the measure of my success as a wife is set free from the chains of human expectations and laid at the foot of the cross to be weighed and measured by the one who loves me most: my Savior, Jesus Christ.

When God created man in his image, he gave him the privilege of having a perfect relationship with his creator. God saw that Adam had no suitable companionship in the Garden of Eden, and he desired that Adam have a partner for fellowship and to work alongside him. None of the creatures that had been created in Eden were measuring up to the needs of Adam, so God did a most amazing thing. He caused Adam to fall asleep and, with just a little organic anesthesia he took from Adam's side a rib from which he fashioned a woman. When Adam awoke and God introduced him to Eve, he was overwhelmed with gladness. The God of the universe created someone who would be the perfect fit for Adam's needs. God knew exactly what men and women would need from each other in every area of our lives, because God is the creator and designer of all of us. So God personally created a relationship that would fulfill those needs. In view of God's perfect design, wouldn't it be wise of us to turn to God's Word to study and learn from it, in order to establish *how* these relationships would work best?

Count the Cost

Whoever does not carry his own cross and come after me cannot be my disciple. For which one of you, when he wants to build a tower, does not first sit down and calculate the cost to see if he has enough to complete it? Otherwise, when he has laid a foundation and is not able to finish, all who observe it begin to ridicule him, saying, 'This man began to build and was not able to finish.' Or what king, when he sets out to meet another king in battle, will not first sit down and consider whether he is strong enough with ten thousand *men* to encounter the one coming against him with twenty thousand? Or else, while the other is still far away, he sends a delegation and asks for terms of peace. So then, none of you can be my disciple who does not give up all his own possessions.

Luke 14:27-33 (NASB)

Great relationships are best when made up of faithful disciples of Christ. Those who have counted the cost and chosen to start building under the direction of the Master Builder himself are ready and equipped to finish the tower. Free to choose, but not free from cost. Have you counted the cost of investing in the life of someone else?

I have been teaching God's word for thirty years to many different ages, but in particular, young adults 18-26 years old. After my experiences in those marriage conferences and reading relationship books that were full of psychology-based survey preferences, I made a vow before God: as long as I have breath and the ability to teach, I would make sure the young men and women that God entrusted to me would learn how to build relationships, grow in love, and marry each other with truths from God's word as the fundamental blueprint. The passion of my life is to see these young men and women equipped and grounded in the Word of God so it will be a lamp to their feet and a light to their path. I want them to memorize God's word, so they won't sin against him in how they conduct these precious relationships. I would remind them that this hidden word in their heart will also enable them to live in the fullness of life that God gives, whether they ever marry or not. I want to celebrate with them as their marriages thrive, and they grow to love each other even more than they ever imagined because it comes from their relationship with Christ. Let's praise him for establishing that covenant relationship with us that makes all of this possible.

Brothers in Christ, choosing to have a standard of Godliness in your dating relationship is going to require a lot from you in discipline, patience, and service. Ephesians 5:25 tells husbands to love their wives just like Christ also loved the church and gave himself up for her. Jesus' plan is not an easy path, calling a man to lead his home by loving his wife, serving her and being willing to die for her. Have you counted that cost?

Sisters in Christ, Ephesians 5:22 teaches wives to be submissive to their husbands, as to the Lord. Here are a few questions she should ask herself before committing to anyone in a dating relationship: Is trusting her husband to lead her and her family an easy response ? Does she respect this man enough to submit to his leadership over her? Is he a man that she will trust to lead and equip their children throughout their lives?

Her personal accountability before God will not be about what kind of husband *he* was, but about her obedience to the plan God has for *her* as his wife. She must surrender her own needs to the Lord and let his plans become her plans.

Tremendous peace and security is present when a girl is willing to wait to date a guy that is trusting God and obeying His commands. Even if such a dating relationship doesn't evolve into marriage, hopefully she has developed a wonderful friendship, and those are truly rare. Be ever so thankful for a Godly friend. If a husband is willing to die for his wife, to sacrifice his life for her like Jesus did for his Bride, which is the Church, maybe a guy needs to first count the cost for building this tower.

Marriage is like a tower. Building this marriage tower will involve patience in dating and will find its completion in a marriage that lasts a lifetime. Does he want to start building this tower beginning with dating and ending with marriage? Has he considered what the cost is to finish this ultimate tower, the marriage tower? Is he committed to following the blueprints that God has established regarding these relationships and how God commands him to love and conduct himself in them? Maybe it is time for every guy to sit down and see if he has what it takes to finish his tower. King David begged the Lord to show him what he needed to change in his life:

> O Lord, You have searched me and known me. You know when I sit down and when I rise up; You understand my thought from afar. You scrutinize my path and my lying down, And are intimately acquainted with all my ways. Search me, O God, and know my heart; Try me and know my anxious thoughts; And see if there be any hurtful way in me, And lead me in the everlasting way.
>
> Psalm 139:1–3, 23–24 (NASB)

That is what this book is about. The purpose is to give guys and girls some tools that are absolutely crucial in the construction and completion of the tower. Find some people around you that love Jesus and are devoted to becoming like him and let them help you build this tower. You need them and they can help you.

Scripture teaches that your days are numbered and only God knows the length of them, so it is urgent that you redeem the time you have on this earth and make it count for eternity. Give God's relationship plan a chance. Considering the pain and lifelong hurt of divorce and multiple broken relationships, surely it can't hurt to give God's plan a try. Could it get any worse than what we see in this pained generation already?

Like a river rising in my soul to share with all those who will listen, here is my primary message—effective, fulfilling and enduring relationships will come when people are first living out their faith in Christ by being obedient to his commands on their life. Great relationships and great marriages cannot depend on the changing preferences of surveys, trendy relationship experts and popular opinions. These preferences will teach guys and girls about the culture they live in, but have crippled them with shallow rules, minimal expectations and flesh-driven requirements.

The Myths
We Are Told

Men of God, I am a fan. God created men to be the head of the household and I am so thankful for that plan. God has designed men in His image and can equip him with all that he needs to fulfill this role. Guys are designed to be more than the sum of a survey. However, he has been so dumbed down through media, music and even some faith-based relationship experts that he just might trip over the proverbial bar that has been set at about his knees. If one more person says that inappropriate, unethical, lustful, rude, thoughtless, ungodly behavior in men should be understood, I am going to scream. Furthermore, if the suggested response to these bad behaviors is that the girlfriend should change something to accommodate his behavior because he is "hard-wired" like that, then we need to flip on the switch of the Light of the World in order to expose the ridiculousness and foolishness of this claim. There are legions of people who want to fight for every guy to be strong and faithful. Girls need to see guys stand firm and be strong in spirit and character so that one day he will take his place as the head of the household and on the front lines of protecting his family. There are guys who can, and will, count the cost for building the tower and find that he *does* have what it takes to finish the construction of it and there are legions of girls who will cheer for them throughout the entire construction process.

The truth is *everyone* is "hard-wired" for bad behavior. It's called sin. Romans 3:23 says everyone has missed the mark that God intended for people. He also teaches that the way people used to think and be motivated must be offered as a sacrifice to him, so that your new desires and motivations are controlled by the Spirit of God. You need to surrender to this plan of God in every area of your life.

This "hard-wired" excuse runs pretty thin. If guys are lusting after girls, it does not mean his girlfriend should start dressing cuter, lose some weight, or workout more so he won't be tempted to lust. A guy is solely responsible for his choices. *Every* individual is responsible for their choices. If lust has taken him captive, then he must repent and stop lusting. God says, "but I say to you that everyone who looks at a woman with lust for her has already committed adultery with her in his heart" Matthew 5:28 (NASB). So, by the mercies of God, don't buy into this spineless philosophy that it is his girlfriend who needs to adjust when he has been caught in sin. Reject the lies that her expectations are too high when she wants faithfulness and integrity in his life. Rebuke the lies that a guy's bad-boy, "hard-wired" behavior should be tolerated and understood.

If a guy is a born-again Christian, his behavior is weighed and measured by the plumb line of God's word alone, not a result of anyone else's survey, opinions or cultural norms. There are guys who don't want God to find them lacking in the spiritual maturity it takes to build a healthy relationship into a lifetime marriage. It's time to grow up. It's time to live out God's commands on your life. Call me crazy, but I think guys and girls want that. God placed within everyone, at creation, the need to be like him because everyone was created in his image. Both have specific needs, and how gracious and perfect is God to also create within them the ability to meet those needs for each other.

A guy must determine in his heart today to fulfill what God has planned for him. A girl needs him to do that. The whole world needs him to fulfill that plan, not due to popular vote, but because it is God's divine order.

A guys transformation from what he used to be and how he used to think can only take place by the power of Almighty God. It's like when babies know only the inside of a warm and safe womb and then *bam!* lights, coldness and a slap on the behind welcome them to this new life in the world! They will see, hear and feel things they never have before. That's what happens when the scales of a guys spiritual eyes are removed. What seemed safe, logical, and predictable changes. These new, unveiled eyes reveal that he has this heart that can be hurt and wounded. But, it also has this enormous capacity for love, favor, commitment, grace, forgiveness, joy and so much more. These attributes are not possible because he has it within his own power to demonstrate them, but because God gives them to him and empowers him to sustain them.

When you give away everything in order to be a disciple, then you begin to take on the characteristics of the only living, one-true God. You have this awareness within you that someone is bigger than you; someone is in control and making provision for you somehow. Maybe that is why the most remote village where no civilized influence has been seen or felt will have a totem pole at the center of their village where people go to worship or a rock carved in the shape of some idol. They seem to have an awareness that there is someone they need to thank and therefore worth worshipping. In Acts 17, the Apostle Paul saw an altar to an "unknown god" when he was traveling through Athens.

> Paul then stood up in the meeting of the Areopagus and said: "People of Athens! I see that in every way you are very religious. For as I walked around and looked carefully at your objects of worship, I even found an altar with this inscription: *to an unknown god.* So you are ignorant of the very thing you worship-and this is

what I am going to proclaim to you. "The God who made the world and everything in it is the Lord of heaven and earth and does not live in temples built by human hands. And he is not served by human hands, as if he needed anything. Rather, he himself gives everyone life and breath and everything else.

Acts 17:22–25 (NASB)

Brothers and Sisters in Christ, you have access to all of God's power as a resource for all matters of your life. Because God is love, you can love. If you have trusted Jesus and committed your life to follow Him, then you have the Holy Spirit within you enabling you to love like he did. When you have counted the cost of trusting Christ and obeying his instructions in all matters of life he will guide you to all truth.

When a girl desires to follow Christ, she should wait for a guy who is pursuing God's plan. She needs to wait for the guy who listens to and learns from those who would point him to Christ as the model for all of his behavior. Her self-imposed timelines of marriage need to be destroyed on the altar of God's perfect timing. "He said to them, 'It is not for you to know times or seasons that the Father has fixed by his own authority" (Acts 1:7). She is so worth waiting for a man who will love her like Jesus does.

This book is designed to help you learn five things—basically five primary disciplines that guys should develop in their lives and for girls to look and wait for in the guys with whom she might enter into a relationship and eventually marry. Don't settle for the character traits that the world has suggested. Those worldly traits are designed to fulfill temporary wants from each other and appeal to the selfish desires of your mind. They seem fulfilling for a season, but ultimately leave you empty and disillusioned.

Because you were created in God's image, you need to go to the source of instruction from the Creator. The Bible reveals how God has designed you and what he requires of you. Keep in mind, if the man that she loves, and thinks she wants to marry, does not have these five disciplines in his life, it doesn't mean he never will. What it does mean is that she needs to wait. Girls, pray for the guy you love—or even better, pray for all guys to desire these disciplines and that God will work in their lives to develop them.

The same is true with a girl's disciplines as well. Her encouragement and respect can urge these great guys to want to grow in Godliness. In this time of life when she is not married, a girl should be focusing on her obedience to the mission that God has given her. She should grow and flourish in a life of surrender to the Savior. Women were created with precision and care. God knew what she would look like and how many hairs would be on her head before she was ever born. She can trust him.

In the future, when you go to a conference or read a book or magazine article about relationships and marriage, ask yourself if what you are being taught is in God's word. Any expectation that is less than God's standard is temporary and may even be counter to a lifetime commitment. Weigh each suggestion and determine if it is a principle or precept from God's Word. If it is lacking in biblical credibility, then cast those expectations out of your mind. Don't waste your time and energy on the pointless and temporary. Wait for the enduring attributes of God himself manifested in a man after God's own heart.

Marriage will always involve a measure of faith. This is a commitment to someone for the rest of your life, so make wise decisions before you ever date someone. Girls should make decisions about who she will date based on the guy's character that she sees lived out before her right now as opposed to hoping he will develop these disciplines later. When she waits for a guy that is displaying these disciplines then she can have a greater confidence through faith that God will sustain their marriage for a lifetime. It's not just a fairytale; lifetime marriages really can happen. Scripture commands it, so God can enable it. Wait for God to do the work.

What about Boaz?

In my request to God for instruction and insight in how to equip the guys in our collegiate ministry to be Godly boyfriends and eventually great husbands, God sent me to the book of Ruth.

God spoke truth into my heart as I was reacquainted with the amazing relationship between Boaz and Ruth. I know these disciplines God pointed out to me are good because God wrote the book. And I know the disciplines demonstrated in the book of Ruth work, because God's ways works.

Ruth grew up in Moab. The family of Elimilech and Naomi moved to Moab from Bethlehem with their sons Mahlon and Chilion because there was a famine in Bethlehem. Ruth met and married Mahlon. His brother Chilion married a woman named Orpah. Tragically, all three of the men, Elimilech, the father, Mahlon and Chilion, all died while in Moab, leaving

Naomi, Ruth and Orpah all widows. After living in Moab for about ten years, Naomi's deep grief and bitterness of heart after losing all of the men in her family caused her to move back to Bethlehem in order to be closer to her family whom she loved. Naomi begged her daughter-in-laws to stay in Moab and find another husband among their people, but Ruth insisted on moving to Bethlehem with her. Ruth felt very committed to Naomi and wanted to help her any way she could. She had also developed a loyalty to the God that Naomi worshipped and served. Jehovah God became her Lord. Her statement of commitment to Naomi has been used in many wedding ceremonies as part of the vows that are made: "But Ruth said, "Do not urge me to leave you or turn back from following you; for where you go, I will go, and where you lodge, I will lodge. Your people shall be my people, and your God, my God." Ruth 1:6 (NASB)

Ruth, herself, is worthy to be studied and learned from; however, it is from the example of Boaz that these five disciplines for guys to incorporate in their life were developed.

> Ram the father of Amminadab, Amminadab the father of Nahshon, Nahshon the father of Salmon, Salmon the father of Boaz, whose mother was Rahab, Boaz the father of Obed, whose mother was Ruth, Obed the father of Jesse, and Jesse the father of King David.
>
> Matthew 1:4–6 (NASB)

Boaz's mother, Rahab, was a prostitute. Imagine that. Right there in the lineage of Christ is a woman that no one would expect to be there. Would anyone believe that a man like Boaz, who the bible teaches in the book of Ruth, loved so purely and was such a respected man in the community—and yes, a man who loved the Lord God so faithfully—would be the son of a prostitute?

The fact that Boaz's mother, Rahab, was a prostitute points us to God's grace, mercy, and unconditional love already. What a glorious message of hope for guys and girls everywhere. No matter the upbringing or lack of instruction in spiritual things, even to the point of your home life being the exact opposite of what God desires it to be, God *can* and *will* redeem it when you put your faith in Him. When Rahab trusted the God of Israel in the book of Joshua, Chapter 2, God turned her whole life around. From a life in the sex industry to finding herself in the lineage of Jesus Christ is such a beautiful picture of the way God works. His redeeming love makes old things in your life pass away, and all things in your life become new.

One of the main reasons I have used the disciplines found in the life of Boaz is that Boaz was a one-woman man. He loved Ruth like every woman wants and needs to be loved. This is a man that foreshadowed Jesus, the one who was to come. He loved Ruth the way Jesus would love us. These are disciplines that every girl needs to know so she can watch for them and *wait* for them to be demonstrated in a guy's life.

I pray every guy will pursue and incorporate these things in their lives as well—not because Boaz had them, but because Jesus does.

When a guy will learn and incorporate these five disciplines in his life then he can see what powerful works God can do in his relationship. A guy should look at his life now. Is he doing what he has been told to do by others, regarding relationships? If he is, how has that plan been working for him? Most importantly, does the Lord see his behavior and say "Well done?"

When guys are living out these five disciplines, or at least getting in the race to develop them, so many of the perpetual complex issues of love and marriage can be resolved. Relationships will be healthy and strong, thriving and uplifting, as well as enabling and enduring when these disciplines are pursued.

A guy must decide if he wants that. Does anyone want that anymore? I think he does.

Please find a Bible—in a church, in your house, on your phone or on your computer—and read the whole book of Ruth. I think you will see why it is their story God picked to teach me these five disciplines. If you should want to know God's "whole story" for your life, not just his message in Ruth, keep reading the Bible. There is good news in the words God wrote. The Bible is one big love story of God's efforts to reach out to you and show you how much he loves you.

The Fundamentals

B efore we begin the five things that are at the heart of this study, there are some prerequisites that you need to understand so that these disciplines will be better implemented in your life.

Fundamental # 1

This is a study of the life of Boaz and how he loved Ruth; however, it is Jesus that you ultimately need to emulate. Boaz is a picture of Jesus. So as you delve into Boaz's life and see these disciplines develop, always be aware that it is because of his love for and obedience to God that these are possible. When a girl wants to wait on someone, she might want to wait on someone like Boaz, but in doing so, who she is really waiting on is someone like Jesus, and that is *always* good.

Fundamental # 2

Understand and be able to define the relationships that you are in. If there is not a clear understanding of how relationships are different, a guy will not know the appropriate way to demonstrate these five disciplines toward the girl in his life.

These levels of relationships are rooted in the understanding that scripture refers to different types of love that God asks us to share. Throughout God's Word we see demonstrated three basic ways we love others:

Agape' – selfless, sacrificial, unconditional love. This is the love God has for us.

> He who has My commandments and keeps them is the one who loves Me; and he who loves Me will be loved by My Father, and I will love him and will disclose Myself to him.

> John 14:21 (NASB)

Philia – close friendship or brotherly love. These relationships are found with family members, close friends, acquaintances, and those you spend a lot of time with.

> Be devoted to one another in brotherly love, give preference to one another in honor;

> Romans 12:10 (NASB)

Eros – the physical, sensual love between a husband and wife that is found in the Old Testament book Song of

Solomon. The love you feel for the one you desire to marry; that romantic love that accompanies agape' love. Knowing how to express this love in the way God intends is imperative in order for you to have the blessings of God on such a relationship.

> Let him kiss me with the kisses of his mouth! For your love is better than wine; your anointing oils are fragrant; your name is oil poured out; therefore virgins love you. Draw me after you; let us run. The king has brought me into his chambers.
>
> Song of Solomon 1:2–4 (NASB)

Knowing these different types of love will help you determine what is appropriate in how you manifest these 5 Things in the different relationships you have. For example, you should not hold hands with or kiss your co-worker if you are dating someone else. You wouldn't shake hands when saying goodnight to your wife like you might do with your dinner guests when they leave. I think you get the idea.

There are three basic levels of relationships based on the three types of love we find in scripture. Not to appear patronizing for the more relationship-savvy people, the reason I am even including these in this book is because over the years of counseling and teaching on relationship principles, I have learned not to assume that everyone has a clear understanding of how to define relationships. When you don't have clear definitions, you make big mistakes, and those usually result in big hurts. Here are the basics:

A. Level 1 = friend, acquaintance, human being

You should demonstrate all 5 Things in these people's lives. Since they are a reflection of the character of Christ, everyone should be a beneficiary in their appropriate forms.

> For God so loved the world, that He gave His only begotten Son, that whoever believes in Him shall not perish, but have eternal life.
>
> John 3:16 (NASB)

> The Lord is not slow about His promise, as some count slowness, but is patient toward you, not wishing for any to perish but for all to come to repentance.
>
> 2 Peter 3:9 (NASB)

B. Level 2 = Someone who is closer to you than a casual acquaintance. You might have years of friendship history, or because they are related to you (sister, mom, grandmother, children), or because you are beginning to date them or considering dating them. This level would include philia and agape' love. Biblical examples of this level of relationship would be Jesus and his mother Mary, Ruth and mother-in-law Naomi, Jesus and his disciples, Jonathan and his dear friend David, Paul and his young ministry partner Timothy,

Mary and her cousin Elizabeth, and Jesus and the family of Mary, Martha and their brother Lazarus.

> Now it came about when he had finished speaking to Saul, that the soul of Jonathan was knit to the soul of David, and Jonathan loved him as himself.
>
> 1 Samuel 18:1 (NASB)

> Now Jesus loved Martha and her sister and Lazarus.
>
> John 11:5 (NASB)

C. Level 3 = only one person can fit in this category, and that will be your spouse, or the one you are dating or engaged to marry. No one should feel the depth, commitment, and full strength of all of the 5 Things more than this one person. This is all of the loves put together exclusively for this one person. You give them every kind of love : agape', philia, and eros. Even within this level, there are boundaries of purity that are required in God's plan. Sexual activity is blessed by God only in the covenant of marriage. There are other expressions of eros love that are appropriate for the one you are dating or engaged. These feelings of romantic love should never be expressed to anyone else.

The only exception we have in loving someone more, according to scripture, is in your relationship with Jesus Christ—which should make all other relationships look pale in comparison. He commands us to love all others (including our spouse) less than we love him.

Fundamental # 3

Know what God's definition of love is and what it looks like. A guy or girl can't just say they love someone and not know how that is put into action. Memorize these truths and incorporate them into your life. When you learn to love like this, you will have the knowledge and thus the tools to *demonstrate* selfless love within all of your relationships The following three areas of biblical truth are the plumb line God gives to measure whether you are or are not authentically loving.

A. God *Is* Love – The Bible teaches us that you know how to love when you know God. Because he *is* love. And the only way to know God is to know Jesus. Jesus says that when you have seen him, you have seen his Father. This makes it clear that in order to truly love someone else, you must love God first. Wait for someone who knows that God is love and loves Jesus, so they can then know how to love you.

> Beloved, let us love one another, for love is from God, and everyone who loves is born of God and knows God. The one who does not love does not know God, for God is love. By this the love of God was manifested in us, that God has sent His only begotten Son into the world so that we might live through Him. In this is love, not that we loved God, but that He loved us and sent His Son to be the propitiation for our sins. Beloved, if God so loved us, we also ought to love

one another. No one has seen God at any time; if we love one another, God abides in us, and His love is perfected in us.

1 John 4:7–12 (NASB)

B. Love *is not*: jealous, prideful, rude, arrogant, wanting your own way, irritable, resentful, being glad when someone is wronged (1 Corinthians 13). These are relationship killers. Know them well. While it is in you to occasionally find these sins felt and demonstrated, be diligent to recognize them as sin. Call them what they are, then seek forgiveness from the one(s) you have wounded with these behaviors. Go before the Lord and ask for forgiveness, mercy and strength to repent and not act out the behavior again. Accountability is a great tool in strengthening this area of discipline.

C. Love *is*: patient with others, kind toward all people, happy when truth is known, able to bear all things you are confronted with, able to believe all things can be used of God and for God, hopeful in all things because your faith is in the one who is your hope, able to endure anything that is put in your path of life whether good or bad, and finally, love never fails. Love from God never quits working, it always accomplishes what God intended it to accomplish. (1 Corinthians 13).

Love is patient, love is kind. It does not envy, it does not boast, it is not proud. It does not dishonor others, it is not self-seeking, it is not easily angered, it keeps no record of wrongs. Love does not delight in evil but rejoices with the truth. It always protects, always trusts, always hopes, always perseveres. Love never fails.

1 Corinthians 13:4–8a (NASB)

Have you got these truths memorized? Anchor them in your heart and meditate on them every day and night. These are fundamental truths that are needed in order to support the five disciplines you are about to get into. This journey is going to be so much fun.

Thing No. 1 Favor

Then Boaz said to Ruth, "Listen carefully, my daughter. Do not go to glean in another field; furthermore, do not go on from this one, but stay here with my maids. Let your eyes be on the field which they reap, and go after them. Indeed, I have commanded the servants not to touch you. When you are thirsty, go to the water jars and drink from what the servants draw." Then she fell on her face, bowing to the ground and said to him, "Why have I found favor in your sight that you should take notice of me, since I am a foreigner?"

Ruth 2:8–10 (NASB)

Favor is a huge thing. For a guy to show a girl favor is to accept her, to choose her for something unique and special. The girl he picks is the one he favors. He will show graciousness toward her and take pleasure in her presence and he *delights* in her. Isn't it wonderful to think of someone delighting in you? Delight has become one of my new favorite words. It is such a remarkable gift for someone to show you favor by taking delight in you. Boaz showed Ruth favor.

Before Boaz ever noticed Ruth, he came home from a trip and greeted his workers with a blessing from God, which established right away his character and the kind of authority figure he was. When he began to look over his fields and saw Ruth for the first time, he asked his workers about her. Yes—he saw her and inquired about her.

It seems things weren't too different back then than they are now, regarding wanting to know about a girl. Boaz was just a good man who saw someone new and wanted to know who she was. How many times has a guy been at a party, an event or even at church, noticed a girl, then turned his back to her so she could not read his lips, and asked a friend, "Ok, who is the girl over there by the chair with the black dress and dark brown hair?" This is what Boaz was doing, even though he was her employer and had good reason to ask about her.

The desire of Ruth's heart was that someone would be gracious enough to allow her to glean the leftover barley in the fields, after the workers had harvested the heartiest stalks of wheat. She hoped someone would say it was okay for her to be there and welcome her to work there. Boaz gave her that favor.

Boaz showed Ruth favor when he told her to "listen carefully" to him. He asked her to not work in any other field, but to stay and work with him. He assured her that she would have work available throughout the duration of the harvest season.

Boaz also told her he would make sure she had everything she needed. She would not lack for anything, because she was special to him and he delighted in her presence. Oh yes, he favored her alright. Then Ruth did something that every girl needs to learn to do. She acknowledged his favor by speaking a word of gratitude.

> "May I continue to find favor in your eyes, my lord," she said. "You have put me at ease by speaking kindly to your servant—though I do not have the standing of one of your servants."

> Ruth 2:13 (NIV)

Ruth pointed out specific ways Boaz had favored her; therefore, affirming his delight toward her. She told him how he made her feel comfortable working for him. He made her feel wanted and welcomed whereever he was. She felt special, and that came from him making her feel safe and comfortable with the crew of workers under his employ.

Girls need to say thank you more often when guys show them acts of favor. If she will start naming the specific acts of kindness, graciousness or delight shown toward her, it may encourage more acts of kindness. It's not a manipulation; it's a word of confirmation. Guys get called out quickly for their acts that girls find gross, rude and inappropriate, so start a movement that thanks guys for their acts of a noble nature, favor and kindness. Name the act specifically so he is clear on what good thing he has done.

Ruth also reminded Boaz of how he spoke kindly to her. Proverbs 18:21 tells us that words are the source of life and death in your spirit, so how much more would it be crucial to speak kind, healing words in the life of the one you are in love with? Boaz always spoke with consideration of Ruth's needs. Kind words are a healing balm. Proverbs 15:1 says words can stop anger and thus change the direction of a bad day. "Kind words are like honey-sweet to the soul and healthy for the body" Proverbs 16:24 (NASB). Guys should want to be the one who causes anger, anxiousness, and fear to disappear from their favored ones life. If he shows her favor through his words, this can be accomplished.

When something great happens, don't you find that you can't wait to tell someone? Ruth was the same way. When she got through working in the fields, the first thing she did when she got home was tell Naomi, her mother-in-law, all of the wonderful things she had experienced since she met Boaz. She showed Naomi all of the leftover food that Boaz sent home with her, as well as the extra wheat she was given. She also reported how he told her to stay with his workers until the whole harvesting season was over. Naomi was so thankful and rejoiced at Ruth's good fortune and blessings. She told Ruth to stay in this man's fields through the whole harvest season and be thankful for God's blessings! Ruth continued to work for Boaz. What a wise girl! What a great spring!

When a man loves a woman, and wants to pursue her, he *must* show her favor. She needs to know that she is favored above all other girls in his life, even his mom. She also needs to know that he favors her over other hobbies and interests he might have as well. Hear me clearly, it is *not* that he should refrain from having any other interests or hobbies. That would be tragic. But, when she knows that no other person or interests in his life take precedence over her, there is a peace and security that resides in her spirit. Favor is when a man creates within a woman a certainty that if he could only pick one person to have with him on a deserted island, he would pick her. Favor is showing her that if she really needed him at home, he would stay and help instead of golf, or hunting or any other option he might have. It's when she knows that if he was asked to pick out the prettiest girl in the room, he would point to her. It is when he chooses her idea over another's. Favor in a healthy, loving home, is a dad showing their children that he and their mother are a united team. Favor shown to a girl can rescue her heart from insecurity and discouragement and establish her feet on a path of contentment and joy.

A girl wants to be clear that she is his favorite. Always. How a guy expresses that favor toward her will look different depending on each guys personality. Relationships can be so much more fulfilling when guys are free to express favor without being compared to another guys expression of favor to the girl he loves. One guy may prefer and delight in bringing a girl flowers and writing a poem. Another guy may show favor by asking her on a date and paying for the meal and the movie, while another may show favor by saving a girl a seat by him at some event. Another way a guy might show favor is to get a big tattoo on his arm of a heart with her name in the middle of it or have her name burned into the back of his leather belt for all to see when he wears his favorite Levi's. Don't you love it? There are as many ways to show favor as there are personalities, and that is one of the many ways that makes life and love so much fun. This leaves absolutely no room for comparison. Often, the death of a guy's desire to show any acts of favor is that he is continually compared to other guys, and thus, quenching his spirit. Let it go. Enjoy the expression of his unique personality and how that will impact the way he shows you his favor.

The underlying principle of favor should always be clear in its expression—that he has made her his favorite, and he delights in showing her that. A girl's willingness to trust a guy with her life, her future, and her heart puts her in a very vulnerable place, so exercising the discipline of favor makes her feel stronger and more secure. She is peaceful and free of fear and anxiety because she is sure that his favor towards her exceeds all things except his relationship with Jesus Christ.

A word of encouragement to those guy's who are fathers or hope to be a father one day. A father's favor toward his daughter is such a cornerstone in her future happiness. A little girl needs to hear her dad tell her how special she is to him. She needs to believe that he thinks she is great, regardless of academic achievement, athletic performances or social status among her peers. The favor a father shows his daughter sets a standard of how she should always be treated in word and deed. When a girl has never experienced favor from her father, she will continue searching for it, and by not really knowing what it is she is needing, may go from one failed relationship to another trying to find that favor that eludes her. If a girl has had an absent or disengaged father, her heart and spirit may not have felt the power of favor and the grace and delight it is designed to bring to her life. Not only is it crippling for girls who have not received favor, but it handicaps young men as well. How will they know how to show favor to anyone when they have not ever seen it modeled by their fathers, or other male authorities in their lives?

Praise God that his grace can fill the void when favor has been absent from the earthly home. God favors you so much! You may have gone through several painful relationships before you realized and understood that favor is good and it comes straight from the heart of God. God has designed girls to need favor, just as He has designed guys to need to give it. Be empowered by the fact that all are created in God's image and God has shown the ultimate favor by making people the object of his affection and delight.

> For thus says the Lord of hosts, "After glory he has sent me against the nations which plunder you, for he who touches you, touches the apple of his eye. For behold, I will wave my hand over them so that they will be plunder for their slaves. Then you will know that the Lord of hosts has sent me.
>
> Zechariah 2:8–9 (NASB)

> As God's co-workers we urge you not to receive God's grace in vain. For he says, "In the time of my favor I heard you, and in the day of salvation I helped you." I tell you, now is the time of God's favor, now is the day of salvation.
>
> 2nd Corinthians 6:1–2 (NIV)

A girl needs to be grounded in the truth that complete favor will only come from her Heavenly Father, and she needs to be confident that he is enough. Her hope should always be in Christ and since marriage is to be a picture of that same hope, favor must be demonstrated in lavish and loving ways from her boyfriend so that she will trust him to show her favor as her husband as well.

For a guy to develop the discipline of favor he must be in the process of growing in Christ and learning to let go of the habits and patterns that rob him of being able to show favor. Until he understands the favor of God, it will be harder for him to show it to others. Maturing in this discipline needs to include some other spiritual disciplines in his life that will enable the Holy Spirit to strengthen him: like Bible study, consistent prayer life, and having an older man of God mentor him and help him grow. Find a mentor who is authentic and real in his favor of others, especially the women in his family and particularly his wife, if he is married.

Girls can know if a guy will show them favor. Watch how he shows favor to the female friends and family members in his life. Are his friends and family members all treated with respect and grace? Are they recipients of kind words? Wait for a guy who is already demonstrating this discipline in his life. Anyone can make a girl feel special for a season, but the guy she needs to marry should be committed to making her feel favored over all else for a lifetime. One of the best ways a girl can have this confidence is seeing him demonstrate it toward her from the beginning of their relationship.

Guys need to consider the levels of relationships we have discussed earlier. In light of these definitions, it must be clear that the general favor shown to other girls in his life is *different* than the favor shown toward the girl that he is pursuing or dating. It takes a spiritually mature guy to show appropriate kindness, comfort, respect, and gentleness to all people; and yet also show the girl you have fallen in love with that she is your priority, your *most* favored one.

For the guys that feel ill-equipped to show favor, there is hope for you. Just read and learn in these particular stories how favor from Jesus Christ changed the lives of these individuals he encountered while here on earth.

Jesus was so gracious to Zaccheus. Here was a man hated by all because of his unscrupulous ways as a tax collector. Tax collecting in that day was characterized by cheating and stealing from those that had no recourse. When Jesus came to his town, Zaccheus climbed up in a tree because he was too short to see over the crowd already lined up to see Jesus walk by. When Jesus got to where Zaccheus was, he looked up at him, called him by name and then invited himself to dinner with Zaccheus. Oh, the favor Zaccheus must have felt. For the Messiah to call him by name and want to come eat at his house, when it is quite possible that no one else could even stand to be around him, must have been like a fresh wind of hope blowing into his soul. The favor Jesus showed Zaccheus evoked a response – and what a response it was.

> When Jesus came to the place, He looked up and said to him, "Zaccheus hurry and come down, for today I must stay at your house." And he hurried and came down and received Him gladly. When they saw it, they all began to grumble, saying, "He has gone to be the guest of a man who is a sinner." Zaccheus stopped and said to the Lord, "Behold, Lord, half of my possessions I will give to the poor, and if I have defrauded anyone of anything, I will give back four times as much." And Jesus said to him, "Today salvation has come to this house, because he, too, is a son of Abraham. For the

Son of Man has come to seek and to save that which was lost."

Luke 19:5–10 (NASB)

Another example is when a woman was caught in the very act of having sex with a married man and was brought out by the religious elite to the center court of the temple where Jesus was talking with a group of people. Those religious elites knew that the law said she must be stoned, so her accusers were curious to see how Jesus would handle this breach of the law. They threw her to the ground in front of Jesus and asked him what he was going to do about this woman caught in sin. I wish I knew what Jesus began to write in the sand that day and if it was those writings that provoked their responses. However, after he finished his first writing on the ground, his profound statement to them was clearly a game changer.

> But Jesus stooped down and with His finger wrote on the ground. But when they persisted in asking Him, He straightened up, and said to them, "He who is without sin among you, let him be the first to throw a stone at her." Again he stooped down and wrote on the ground. When they heard it, they began to go out one by one, beginning with the older ones, and He was left alone, and the woman, where she was, in the center of the court. Straightening up, Jesus said to her, "Woman, where are they? Did no one condemn you?"

> She said, "No one, Lord." And Jesus said, "I do not
> condemn you, either. Go. From now on sin no more.
>
> John 8:6b–11 (NASB)

This story grips my soul every time I read it. To be sure, she was a sinner and guilty of the crime she was accused of, but Jesus' favor brought her deliverance when the accusors wanted destruction. When the favor of Jesus collides with your sin, it brings deliverance from your sin and not your destruction. How can we ever fully grasp the favor of forgiveness of sin? I'm not sure we can, but I am so thankful Jesus offers it to everyone. Especially me.

Another man that would never forget the favor of God was a man Jesus and his disciples met that had been born blind. Jesus' disciples asked him whose sin had caused the man's blindness—his mother's or his father's? Jesus said that no one's sin had caused the blindness, but that the man was born blind for the purpose of God having an opportunity to demonstrate his power.

> Jesus answered, "It was neither that this man sinned,
> nor his parents; but it was so that the works of God
> might be displayed in him. We must work the works of
> Him who sent Me as long as it is day; night is coming
> when no one can work. While I am in the world, I am
> the Light of the world." When He had said this, He
> spat on the ground, and made clay of the spittle, and
> applied the clay to his eyes, and said to him, "Go, wash

in the pool of Siloam" (which is translated, Sent). So he went away and washed, and came back seeing.

John 9:3–7 (NASB)

The favor of Jesus can heal when the whole world says it can never happen. A man *born* blind had his sight restored because Jesus found him and showed him favor by giving him sight for the first time in his life. Favor brings hope to the hopeless.

There are so many more people that saw, first hand, the favor of God: Abraham, Esther, the woman at the well in Samaria, Lazarus, Mary Magdalene and countless others. He told them all in word or deed that he took pleasure in loving them. He wanted them to know and wants you to know, that you are favored by him. He delights in you and has made a way for you to know him. He desires to have fellowship with you because you are loved and therefore favored.

> They said, "Believe in the Lord Jesus, and you will be saved, you and your household."

Acts 16:31 (NASB)

Even a guy's best demonstrations of favor pale in the shadow of the Redeemer and his choosing to bring grace, healing, hope, forgiveness and salvation to a people that were lost. Praise God for the favor of his son! Praise God that Jesus modeled for everyone a perfect example of favor. And praise

God that every guy has available to him the resources to show favor and it not be left up to his own abilities and experience.

> A good man will obtain favor from the Lord, but he will condemn a man who devises evil.
>
> Proverbs 12:2 (NASB)

> He who finds a wife finds a good thing and obtains favor from the Lord.
>
> Proverbs 18:22 (NASB)

Thing No. 2 Provision

When you are thirsty, go to the water jars and drink from what the servants draw."

Ruth 2:9b (NASB)

At mealtime Boaz said to her, "Come here, that you may eat of the bread and dip your piece of bread in the vinegar." So she sat beside the reapers; and he served her roasted grain, and she ate and was satisfied and had some left.

Ruth 2:14 (NASB)

When she rose to glean, Boaz commanded his servants, saying, "Let her glean even among the sheaves, and do not insult her. Also you shall purposely pull out for her some grain from the bundles and leave it that she may glean, and do not rebuke her.

Ruth 2:15–16

Now, my daughter, do not fear. I will do for you whatever you ask,

Ruth 3:11a

Again he said, "Give me the cloak that is on you and hold it." So she held it, and he measured six measures of barley and laid it on her. Then she went into the city. When she came to her mother-in-law, she said, "How did it go, my daughter?" And she told her all that the man had done for her. She said, "These six measures of barley he gave to me, for he said, 'Do not go to your mother-in-law empty-handed.

Ruth 3:15–17

The second discipline every guy needs to demonstrate and every girl needs to wait for is *provision* – the basic ability and desire to provide for the needs of the ones you love: family, friends and and the girl you love. Boaz provided the needs of Ruth, her mother-in-law, and others employed by him. He was a giver of what he had worked for and earned.

There are two particular ways that we saw Boaz provide for Ruth.

Public Provision

Public provision was his open, public demonstration of provision for those he loved. First, he provided her a job. Though she had been hired by his overseers before he arrived at the fields, he allowed her not only to stay for that season, but provided her a job throughout both of the harvest seasons. Ruth would typically be left to gather the little that was available after the harvesters had gone over the field and definitely not assured of a job during the next harvest. But, Boaz assured her of both – stay here for the remainder of this season and come back for the next one as well. What a generous provision he made for her.

Ruth was also provided for in a public way when he invited her to eat with him at lunch and made sure she had all she wanted. He sent leftovers home with Ruth for Naomi and her, as well as those working in his fields

Provision involves giving from what you have. Generosity with what God has provided for you is a way to say thank you to the Lord as well as to bring glory to him. "Let your light shine before men in such a way that they may see your good works, and glorify your Father who is in heaven." Matthew 5:16 (NASB). Public provision is a way in which a guy demonstrates to others how much he loves the girl that he favors. Appropriate public displays of provision are just showing love to someone by providing what they need.

A few years ago I was teaching these principles at a retreat for junior high and high school girls. Teaching these disciplines to high school girls was fun and fairly easy because they are at an age where it is not a huge leap to make the connection between their stage of life and thinking about the guy they want to marry. They are thinking about marriage already. However, I was worried a little bit about making the transfer of these principles to those girls that were in junior high. Some of them were twelve years old, and hopefully not thinking too much about who they were going to marry. But, the truth is I wanted it to work because it would be an opportunity to be *preventive* of many of the traps the world has waiting for them when they do begin to date. If they could understand what these disciplines mean and how they might be appropriately demonstrated by guys at their age, then they would be much more equipped to make good decisions in the future.

When the junior high girls came to my session I began to explain each of these five disciplines that they needed to look for and appreciate in their guy friends. When I got to provision, I asked them if they could give me some examples of how a young guy their age might provide for them in an age appropriate way. Immediately one young girl, a sixth grader, said, "Well, the other day I was on my way to my locker and dropped all of my books in the hallway. Then Blake Jones ran over to me and started picking them up for me and offered to carry them to my locker for me." I cheered and told her that was exactly what I was talking about. I asked her if she thanked him for helping her, and she said she had. At that time another young girl, another sixth grader, added that she remembered a time when it was pouring down rain and she had gotten her clothes wet and began telling her friends that she was cold. This same 'Blake Jones' came and offered his jacket to her saying he didn't really want to wear it anyway, and she was welcome to borrow it for the rest of the day. Immediately I asked them who in the world was 'Blake Jones' and to tell me who his parents are so I can call them and give them some kind of parenting award!

What I learned that day is that God does indeed put it in our hearts to need things and to want to provide things. You don't have to be an adult to "get it". This young man clearly had this discipline modeled for him by someone in his life and he was just doing what he had learned was the right thing – to provide for someone who has a need if you have the resources to meet that need. Well done, 'Blake Jones,' and well done sixth grade girls for recognizing greatness. (Blake Jones is not his real name of course).

Private Provision

In my opinion, one of the most romantic scenes in Ruth was when Boaz instructed his workers to pull some of the best stalks of grain from their bundles and leave them on the ground for Ruth to pick up during her gleaning time. He provided his very best for her! Ruth was so favored. Without Ruth knowing, he graciously made sure she had access to more than just what would be left over. In doing this Boaz made it clear to those working for him that Ruth was indeed highly favored. While this was a private provision for Ruth in that she did not know this scheme had been formed, it was a public provision witnessed by others.

There have been many conversations about the purpose of private provision and why that might have been Boaz's course of action. Some of the thoughts expressed were that it was possibly a way to help Ruth not feel obligated in any way to repay him, or maybe he knew the potential for jealousy and division due to him showing Ruth favor among the workers and so he didn't want to put her in a precarious and dangerous situation.

Private provision can eliminate conflict with others. Boaz's provision for Ruth seemed to be born out of his genuine care for her. His faithfulness to God provoked a desire to meet the needs of people, and because he favored Ruth, maybe Boaz just delighted in seeing her joy after receiving the blessing of the extra. So a few good reasons to provide privately: eliminate conflict among the group a girl is in, prevent jealousy which can impact her life in a negative way, avoid a perceived need to repay and therefore circumvent the "I owe him something" mindset, and because often it brings a guy joy to provide for her needs without getting the glory, but only to see the surprise and happiness it brings to her life.

When a guy finds joy in providing needs and wants in others' lives, he finds that his capacity to show favor through provision is more than he ever dreamed. To provide great or small things for the one he loves, just because he can, is actually an act of gratitude to the Lord. I have seen and heard testimonies of guys leaving a sweet note on a girl's windshield, or he secretly payed her rent. One guy brought home dinner and had her apartment clean when she got home from work. Other guys have made arrangements to have flowers waiting on her desk at work, or put extra money in her purse before a trip. One of the most generous acts of provision was when one guy gave his girlfriend all of his french fries just because he knew she loved them.

When guys are learning how to implement these disciplines, it is often best to start practicing with the girls that are friends in their life right now. A guy can help if her car is in need of repair, and she needs a ride somewhere. She might need help with a class she is taking or in an academic subject he excels in. Provision is not just about *paying* for something.

In order to prevent any misunderstanding between the guys and the girls in why these acts of provision are being made, there have been guys that worked in groups who have washed cars, left encouraging notes and then all of the guys signed the card saying it was from all of them. Groups of guys have bought dinner for several of their female friends and let them have a 'girls night out'. They delighted in making provision, but didn't want anyone to think there was some hidden agenda behind their efforts. This should resonate in every guy's spirit when it is done because he is created and designed to provide, not because Boaz did, but because God did it first.

Boaz also provided privately for Ruth and Naomi when Ruth went to the barn where Boaz was working to let him know she was willing to marry him. Boaz provided a coat full of barley for her to take home for Naomi and herself. This was a private showing of love and provision and thus favor toward Ruth. When she got home and Naomi asked what Boaz said to her, she reported that he said, "I will take care of you *and* your mother-in-law" and "these six measures of barley he gave to me, for he said, 'Do not go to your mother-in-law empty-handed'" (Ruth 3:16–17).

Can you imagine how this profoundly impacted Ruth's heart since she was the sole caregiver of her mother-in-law? When a guy truly loves a girl, he must be willing to provide for who she must provide for as well when they get married. If she is a widow or a single mom, he wants to help provide for her children. If she has a sick parent, he wants to help ease the burden of her responsibility. Should she have a sister or brother unable to care for themselves or who has fallen on hard times, this just provides another way for him to love her through providing help for those in her life. A guy just gives, helps and provides because he can, and he can because God gave all he had to help and provide for him.

"And my God will supply all of your needs according to His riches in glory in Christ Jesus."

Philippians 4:19 (NASB)

I have been young and now I am old, yet I have not seen the righteous forsaken or his descendants begging bread.

Psalm 37:25

Thing No. 3 Protection

Let your eyes be on the field which they reap, and go after them. Indeed, I have commanded the servants not to touch you.

Ruth 2:9a (NASB)

When she rose to glean, Boaz commanded his servants, saying, "Let her glean even among the sheaves, and do not insult her.

Ruth 2:15 (NASB)

So she lay at his feet until morning and rose before one could recognize another; and he said, "Let it not be known that the woman came to the threshing floor."

Ruth 3:14 (NASB)

Guys are designed by God to protect. Boaz demonstrated for us how far reaching the discipline of protection can be. This protection is a discipline that the Holy Spirit of God develops in a guy in order to manifest the image of God in which he was created.

Protection is especially crucial in the life of the girl a guy is committing his life to in marriage. The consequences of a girl left feeling unsafe, in any area of her life, can have crippling effects. In the story of Boaz and Ruth, we learn three particular areas of Ruth's life in which he protected her.

1. Boaz protected her *body* – he commanded the men working for him not to touch her. Ruth, being a field laborer, as well as a foreigner in his fields, was an easy target and very vulnerable to the unscrupulous ways of the men around her. Although it's hard to imagine that any of the women would be susceptible to evil and perverted behavior from men while employed by a man such as Boaz, he still made sure Ruth was shielded from any inappropriate advances or harm. It is significant that he not only commanded his male workers not to touch her, but he told Ruth that he had secured her protection as well. She was, therefore, able to work with peace and confidence that no one would bring her harm.

   A guy who loves, and thus protects, *never* hits a girl. He walks on the "street side", he holds her arm or hand when in a crowd to keep her safely close to him. A guy who protects will walk ahead and guide her when in a tense or dangerous situation. A guy's need to protect compels him to rush to her if her car is broken down or wrecked to ensure she is safe. A protector will stand between a mom and a rebellious child who is threatening bodily harm. He will answer the knock on the door when it is late at night in order to protect his family. He might even go to war to ensure she will live in safety and free from those who might threaten that peace. These noble protectors will take bullets, stop criminals, run into burning buildings, climb mountains, run into hurricanes and dive into the swelling tides to save people he loves— even to save someone he doesn't know. He is designed by God to protect. That's how he loves.

Another way guys can protect their favored one physically, is by not being promiscuous. This is not done just for her physical protection, but because that is what God requires, and doing so is an act of obedience. The Bible is clear that "Marriage is to be held in honor among all, and the marriage bed is to be undefiled; for fornicators and adulterers God will judge." Hebrews 13:4 (NASB) Having multiple sexual partners does *not* protect the physical health of a guy's future wife. On the contrary, it clearly puts her at great risk of contracting sexually transmitted diseases.

A guy also protects by not having sex with his girlfriend before he is married to her. If a guy is going to be a protector, he must start with protecting a girl from the lust of his own flesh. He should not tempt her to compromise her obedience to the commands of God's word to keep herself pure. The Bible says "Flee from sexual immorality. All other sins a person commits are outside the body, but whoever sins sexually, sins against their own body." 1 Corinthians 6:18 (NIV)

If the command for sexual purity has already been violated, the great news is that God can redeem the sin against the body. God's forgiveness is made possible by the blood shed on the cross. There is hope for a great future if one repents and begins to walk in the life of faithfulness and obedience. God's Word promises that "If we confess our sins, he is faithful and just and will forgive us our sins and purify us from all unrighteousness" (1 John 1:9, NIV).

One of the most profound examples I have heard regarding the impact of protection came from a speaker at a human trafficking conference. Cassie Hammett, our speaker, is the director of the Hub Ministry in Shreveport, Louisiana. A division of this ministry focuses on the rescue of women from the sex trade industry. She told of a time when she and her husband were called in to the police station one night to help a woman who had been taken off the street. She was trembling and shaking with fear because of the threats that were made against her by her pimp. They decided to take her with them in order to ensure her safety. After they placed her in the backseat of their car, they began to drive around while deciding where she should stay for the night. Cassie shared how this young woman was so anxious, fearful, and frantically looking around to see if anyone was following them. Hearing her cries and seeing her anxious behavior, her husband stopped the car and turned around to face her. With great resolve and gentleness, he looked straight in her eyes and told her that she did not need to be afraid anymore. He assured her that those men could not hurt her now. If they tried, they would have to go through him first to get to her, and that wasn't going to happen. The confirmation of the impact of this discipline came when Cassie told the crowd that she had never been more attracted to her husband than in that moment, watching him vow to protect a vulnerable and scared young woman. This is how a guy can speak transforming words and perform life-changing acts of protection when he is empowered by the indwelling Holy Spirit of God.

While guys are powerful protectors, girls have been in the position of needing to protect as well. Many times she has done it with selfless passion and supernatural strength. Several stories in the Bible illustrate this amazing ability of girls to protect.

Genesis 16 tells how Hagar, after being kicked out of the camp she was living in, protected her baby son, Ishmael, from the desert prey, believing her son would surely die. She was waving away animals and vultures and placing her body over him in order to keep the blazing sun from parching his little body. A mother's protection is fierce. God saved him from harm and enabled them to get to safety.

1 Samuel, chapter 25 tells how Abigail's husband, Nabal, refused to help King David with some of the needed supplies for his soldiers. This refusal incurred the wrath of the King. Nabal's inability to protect his family came as a result of his perpetual drunkenness. Abigail's wise, humble, yet bold intervention on behalf of her family before the King and his soldiers spared her family and all of their land from the imminent destruction.

When a law was enacted with the explicit purpose of persecuting and killing the Jews who lived in the country, Queen Esther decided she would risk death in order to save her people. In the book named after her, scripture suggests that God had possibly brought her to this important position for "just such a time as this." Esther was fearless in her desire to protect her people by approaching her husband, the king, without being summoned, which was against the law. Esther spoke to him on behalf of her people and opposed the new edict that would put her people in peril. Because he valued and honored Esther, the king changed the law to protect her people.

In the second chapter of Exodus, Jochabed, mother of Moses, protected him from the death threats of Pharaoh by creating a waterproof basket for Moses to float in down the river as a way of escape. Jochabed had Moses's sister, Miriam, follow and watch as the little basket floated down the river, so she could protect him, if needed, as well as see what happened to him. Ironically, Pharaoh's own daughter saw the basket floating by and rescued him.

There is a common thread here. People who were loved were fiercely and courageously protected. So carry on, woman of God! Protection of those she loves is a manifestation of the image of God in her life. All of these people were protected because a holy God intervened.

2. Boaz protected her *spirit*. Remember how Boaz, in his provision for Ruth, asked his workers to drop some of the best stalks of grain on the ground for her on purpose without her knowing it? He also commanded them to not embarrass or humiliate her when she would begin to pick up these stalks that were clearly not the remnants she was supposed to gather. He saw the potential for her to be humiliated and made sure to protect her spirit. What an ugly scene it would have been had they started yelling out to her and fussing at her for picking up portions of grain she had no right to gather. Boaz was thinking about her spirit and wanted to protect it from being wounded. When a guy has a favored one, she should be protected

from being embarrassed, ridiculed, or demeaned by anyone, especially her protector. It is a guy's obligation to see that no one brings harm to her spirit when it is within his power.

The human spirit is a powerful, yet vulnerable part of every person. The book of wisdom teaches, "A joyful heart is good medicine, But a broken spirit dries up the bones." Proverbs 17:22 (NIV) When there is someone he loves, he will want to protect the place in a girl's life that holds hope, faith, and love—which is her spirit.

The Holy Spirit indwelling us is the greatest power a person can have. His presence enables one to endure, overcome, and thrive when there has been someone who wounded their spirit. In my twenty-five years of ministry to college students, as well as women and youth, I have heard testimony after testimony that bears witness to the fact that a broken spirit is one of the most debilitating conditions of life. It seems to be just as hard to overcome a broken spirit as any physical abuse they may have endured at the hands of boyfriends, fathers or other relatives.

He heals the brokenhearted, and binds up their wounds. He counts the number of the stars; He gives names to all of them. Great is our Lord and abundant in strength; His understanding is infinite.

Psalm 147:3–5

Girls—wait for the guy who protects your spirit. If he is the source of criticism, ridicule, or sarcasm either privately, or in front of others, I implore you to reconsider your relationship with him. There are guys who want to be like Christ. They long to love someone by using words of kindness and they want to speak words of strength and encouragement into your spirit. Look for this guy; wait for him. I know these guys are out there, because I have met many of them and they are waiting for you, too!

3. Boaz protected her *character*. According to Jewish custom at the time, Ruth would present herself to Boaz in such a manner as to let him know she was willing to marry him. It was late at night when she went to see him, and he had already fallen asleep. When he discovered her there, Ruth let her intentions be known, and they discussed their future together. It was still dark when they finished their talk, but in the early morning hours. Boaz knew that he must protect Ruth's character from unfounded rumors about any appearance of immoral behavior. Before she left he instructed the workers not to tell anyone that she had been there and to help get her out of the barn without anyone seeing her. Boaz took this action not to hide something she had done wrong, but to protect her character from assault in spite of what she had done right.

One way guys must protect girls is to stop engaging in inappropriate and vulgar conversations about girls.

Rebuke the ungodly conversations that compromise the reputation of girls, as well as the character destruction that can come from the lips of other guys. God forbid these conversations come from the lips of guys who proclaim the name of Christ. "Let the words of my mouth and the meditation of my heart be acceptable in Your sight, O Lord, my rock and my Redeemer." Psalm 19:14 (NASB) It is time for guys to repent before the Lord and find victory over this sinful behavior. As a defender of her character, a guy can be the wall of protection around a girl when conversations around him become toxic, demeaning, and harmful to her reputation. Be bold, be vigilant. And, may every single guy choose his words with salt by speaking up and putting an end to the conversations that may damage, compromise, or even ruin the character of one of the girls God designed him to protect.

Isn't it interesting that man's first job in the garden was to protect and look after all living things that were placed there? It was a safe place for all living things. If a girl is protected, then there is no fear for her to dream and to enjoy the journey of life God has created for her. Her protection is fundamentally in the hands of an all powerful God, but knowing that her husband is going to protect her gives her tremendous additional peace.

Jesus protected a woman caught in adultery in John 8:1–11. Even though she was guilty of the sin, Jesus stood between her and the mob. When he called them out on their own sin, the accusers and onlookers all walked away. Only one man was left standing by her after the crowd left that day - Jesus. It is a powerful truth that the only one left standing there was the only one who could forgive her, restore her, and love her like no other. That agape' love is so perfect and so unconditional. It should bring deep and profound hope that the ultimate protector is Jesus. He protected her *body* from being stoned to death. He protected her *spirit* when he asked, "Where are your accusers?" and she replied, "There are none here, sir." and he proclaimed, "Then neither do I accuse you. Now, go on home and stop sinning." He also protected her *character* by literally standing up for her, causing the mob to realize they were sinners as well. He became the great equalizer and saved her character. What a gracious and merciful protector God is!

No matter what sinful acts, moral failures, or personal disgrace someone has brought on themselves—it is great to be reminded that the Savior is a protector. He will never "leave you or forsake you", but will guide and instruct in repentance and restoration. He takes lives out of the crippling mud pit and puts them securely on solid ground. Praise God!

> He brought me up out of the pit of destruction, out of the miry clay, And He set my feet upon a rock making my footsteps firm.
>
> Psalm 40:2 (NASB)

Pray that every guy will find that obedience to this discipline of protection will strengthen his spirit, his resolve, and his desire to protect the body, the spirit, and the character of the girl he loves. If a guy has failed to do this, then repentance and asking forgiveness is a first step in his getting back in right relationship with the Lord then obeying what God has commanded him to do. Then he can begin the journey of restoring trust and security. Girls need a guy's protection, and his love for her is demonstrated in how he protects her.

Thing No. 4 Affirmation

Boaz replied to her, "All that you have done for your mother-in-law after the death of your husband has been fully reported to me, and how you left your father and your mother and the land of your birth, and came to a people that you did not previously know. May the Lord reward your work, and your wages be full from the Lord, the God of Israel, under whose wings you have come to seek refuge."

Ruth 2:11–12 (NASB)

Then he said, "May you be blessed of the Lord, my daughter. You have shown your last kindness to be better than the first by not going after young men, whether poor or rich. Now, my daughter, do not fear. I will do for you whatever you ask, for all my people in the city know that you are a woman of excellence.

Ruth 3:10–11a (NASB)

A ffirmation, according to the Merriam Webster dictionary, means to say that something is true in a confident way, to show a strong belief in or dedication to.

The Apostle Paul has a word that he wants us to always speak with confidence,

> This is a trustworthy statement; and concerning these things I want you to speak confidently, so that those who have believed God will be careful to engage in good deeds. These things are good and profitable for men.

> Titus 3:8 (NASB)

The fourth thing guys can learn from Boaz, is *affirmation*. Affirmations come when he speaks in agreement with something he has seen in someone else's life that puts a seal on that behavior. It is a statement of support for whatever someone is doing or saying. Affirmation also involves the discipline of listening and observing so he can find those points in which he can affirm someone.

Boaz affirms Ruth in several areas of her life.

1. Boaz affirms Ruth's *ministry* and *service*. When Boaz first saw Ruth, he asked his workers about her. The report they gave him was about her care and love for Naomi, her mother-in-law. They told him about her willingness to move from the land of her people in Moab, and all that was familiar to her there, to Bethlehem so she could

care for Naomi. Not only did the workers affirm Ruth when they gave such a good report, but Boaz affirmed Ruth when he shared those gracious reports with her personally, therefore affirming her ministry and service before God.

This affirmation could also secure Ruth's desire to continue her ministry and service to the Lord. That is the power of affirmation.

Affirmation is a blessing and encouragement that helps keep one living life with their eyes focused on the eternal things of God, especially when life gets difficult and challenging. The power of affirmation in ministry and what is done to serve others can spur on more service. However, it is not the *need* for affirmation that one must have in order to obey the commands of Christ, but because the pleasure of God is enough. It is in *giving* affirmative statements that the obedience to God's word is realized.

2. Boaz affirmed Ruth's *sacrificial love* for Naomi. Not only did Ruth move back to Bethlehem with Naomi, but her tireless, valiant efforts to provide food for Naomi and herself were well noted and affirmed.

3. Boaz affirmed Ruth's *faith* by commenting on the fact that she had taken refuge under the hand of the one true God. He was encouraged by their mutual faith. Dependence on God for all of her needs was also affirmed in Ruth's life.

When Ruth vowed that Naomi's God would become her God and that she would serve him also, Ruth's faith came alive and was invested in Jehovah God. Boaz saw this faith lived out in her life, so he affirmed her by speaking to her about how he had witnessed her faith to be real and authentic. Affirmations that confirm your faith walk help you keep your eyes fixed on Jesus, the author and finisher of your faith. (Hebrew 12:2)

4. Boaz affirmed Ruth's *integrity* and *graciousness*. He affirmed her decision to choose him as her husband. Boaz knew she could have chosen someone younger and either richer or poorer than he was. He knew that she chose beyond what her eyes could see, and settled on what God had led her to do. He affirmed Ruth by blessing her for her integrity, graciousness and kindness.

Jesus affirms people as well. It is amazing that the King of Kings, the Savior of the world, the perfect, spotless Lamb of God can find attributes in his people that he too takes notice of and affirms. What a great mystery—this presence of God and how he knows all, and sees all, and is everywhere all the time. It is hard to grasp that he can see one act of kindness or one sacrificial act expressed by one person. But, he does –

> And when Jesus entered Capernaum, a centurion came to Him, imploring Him, and saying, "Lord, my servant is lying paralyzed at home, fearfully

tormented." Jesus said to him, "I will come and heal him." But the centurion said, "Lord, I am not worthy for You to come under my roof, but just say the word, and my servant will be healed. For I also am a man under authority, with soldiers under me; and I say to this one, 'Go!' and he goes, and to another, 'Come!' and he comes, and to my slave, 'Do this!' and he does it." Now when Jesus heard this, He marveled and said to those who were following, "Truly I say to you, I have not found such great faith with anyone in Israel.

Matthew 8:5–10 (NASB)

Jesus affirmed the faith of a woman who believed if she could just touch the hem of his coat, she would be healed.

And a woman who had been suffering from a hemorrhage for twelve years, came up behind Him and touched the fringe of His cloak; for she was saying to herself, "If I only touch His garment I will get well." But Jesus turning and seeing her said, "Daughter, take courage; your faith has made you well." At once the woman was made well.

Matthew 9:20–22 (NASB)

Jesus asked the disciples who people thought he was. Then he asked them who *they* thought he was. Simon Peter replied that he believed he was the Christ, the Son of the living God. Jesus affirmed Peter's proclamation by blessing him with a great responsibility.

And Jesus said to him, "blessed are you, Simon Barjona, because flesh and blood did not reveal this to you, but My Father who is in heaven. I also say to you that you are Peter, and upon this rock I will build My church; and the gates of Hades will not overpower it. I will give you the keys of the kingdom; and whatever you bind on earth shall have been bound in heaven, and whatever you loose on earth shall have been loosed in heaven."

Matthew 16:17–19 (NASB)

He affirmed his love for children and their simple faith by proclaiming that anyone who receives a child in his name, receives him.

Sitting down, Jesus called the Twelve and said, "Anyone who wants to be first must be the very last, and the servant of all." He took a little child whom he placed among them. Taking the child in his arms, he said to them, "Whoever welcomes one of these little children in my name welcomes me; and whoever welcomes me does not welcome me but the one who sent me.

Mark 9:35–37 (NIV)

When Jesus went to visit his friends Mary, Martha and Lazarus, Mary wanted to sit in the room and just talk to Jesus and hear what all he had to say. Martha was concerned with making sure the dinner was ready and that the preparations were in order for everyone to eat. Jesus affirmed Mary for choosing to visit with him instead of tending to other things in the house, like her sister Martha, by telling her she had chosen the *best* thing.

> Now as they were traveling along, He entered a village; and a woman named Martha welcomed Him into her home. She had a sister called Mary, who was seated at the Lord's feet, listening to His word. But Martha was distracted with all her preparations; and she came up to Him and said, "Lord, do You not care that my sister has left me to do all the serving alone? Then tell her to help me." But the Lord answered and said to her, "Martha, Martha, you are worried and bothered about so many things; but only one thing is necessary, for Mary has chosen the good part, which shall not be taken from her.
>
> Luke 10:38–42 (NASB)

It is so clear. Jesus Christ, the Savior and Redeemer, taught how to affirm by affirming others himself! He does notice, and he is delighted when he sees his children choosing what brings him glory and honor. Rejoice in the affirmations of the Lord!

So how does a guy affirm his favored one—the one he truly loves? He would make statements of fact regarding her character, just like Boaz did and just like Jesus does. A guy who affirms will tell a girl when he sees her demonstrate kindness, compassion, honesty, gentleness, patience, forgiveness, or a selfless act. Has he seen her return good to some-one who has been evil to her? If he has seen these acts that reflect the nature of Christ, a guy should be quick to share that observation with a girl and affirm those characteristics of Jesus. Did he see her love people no matter if they were difficult or easy to love? Has he heard her praying for people? If she is a mother, a guy should affirm her Godly instruction and encouragement toward her children. Is she teaching others the ways of God by the testimony of her life? Guys can declare these affirmations publicly so others can see his devotion to her and esteem her as well.

It is always a blessing when a guy will share the affirmations with a girl privately too. The personal, private affirmations reach to the depths of her heart because of the intimacy that comes when you share something face to face. Sometimes that can encourage her to desire to be more like Christ and thus have the capacity to love even more. Statements that are whispered only to her like "I have never been as proud as I am right now, to have you sitting next to me" or "Every time I see you working with children I can tell that is what God has called you to do." Other affirmations might be seen in her work ethic or her ability to endure hard times and be patient with difficult people. Then there are statements like King Lemuel's mother taught him to say to the one that he would choose, "many women do noble things, but you surpass them all" (Proverbs 31:29, NIV). Those are empowering words.

Girls need to wait for the guy who *affirms* her; she needs this. She will *never* outgrow needing to be affirmed by the guy that professes to love her.

Other character traits for guys to notice and affirm are the ways she has loved him. Has she trusted him and depended on him because she believed he was able to do a certain task? Has she remembered special things that he loves and worked to provide them for him? Will she allow him to favor her, protect her or provide for her? A guy can attest to these truths and speak to her the affirmations that she needs to hear and he needs to say. Boaz affirmed and Jesus affirmed, so he can, too.

I have a special word of encouragement to girls who did not have a father or any male authority figure in her life who affirmed her worth, talent, skills, character, or her beauty. Everyone needs to know that Psalm 139 teaches that the God of the universe put every part of her body together with purpose. God knows how many hairs are on her head. He created her in his image. Yes, she is made like the Creator of the universe! Romans 5:8 says that he loved her so much that even when he knew she would sin, he died for her anyway. John 15:13 assures her that there is no greater love than when someone lays down his life for a friend, and Jesus did just that! Trust Jesus! Follow Jesus! Give your life to Jesus! He will always be enough. His affirmations will always be true and authentic. His Holy Spirit living in her will equip her with spiritual gifts to serve others with purpose and power.

He produces fruit in her life that can actually enable her to change the world as well as bring hope to someone who is discouraged and broken hearted. "But the fruit of the Spirit is love, joy, peace, patience, kindness, goodness, faithfulness, gentleness, self-control; against such things there is no law." (Galatians 5:22–23 NASB) Her obedience and a life driven by God's truth is her affirmation of who he is, what he does and how much he loves her. "Let your light shine before men in such a way that they may see your good works, and glorify your Father" (Matthew 5:16, NASB).

Girls—praise and encourage the guys who are affirming the people in their life. Lord knows there has been enough pointing out all of his weaknesses and failures and sin. Give him blessings for developing the discipline of affirmation when he speaks. Just saying "thank you" is a great way to start. Tell these guys 'thank you' when you hear him affirming girls, any girls, regarding their character and nature and not on her body or physical appearance.

Praise the Lord there *are* guys who are raising the bar of acceptable behavior to a level of Godliness in how they treat girls. Some guys are not falling into the shallow, temporary, self-serving trap that the world would like for them to stay bound. Be quick to give him a word of encouragement and affirmation as well. Silence for the shallow and words of praise for the behaviors that need to be permanent go a long way.

Thing No. 5 Integrity

Now it is true I am a close relative; however, there is a relative closer than I. Remain this night, and when morning comes, if he will redeem you, good; let him redeem you. But if he does not wish to redeem you, then I will redeem you, as the Lord lives. Lie down until morning."

Ruth 3:12–13 (NASB)

So I thought to inform you, saying, 'Buy it before those who are sitting here, and before the elders of my people. If you will redeem it, redeem it; but if not, tell me that I may know; for there is no one but you to redeem it, and I am after you.'" And he said, "I will redeem it."

Ruth 4:4 (NASB)

So Boaz took Ruth, and she became his wife, and he went in to her. And the Lord enabled her to conceive, and she gave birth to a son.

Ruth 4:13 (NASB)

Bottom line—if a guy's integrity has been lost in his relationship, none of the first four things will have much credibility. The big question is, is he really who he has led people to think he is? Do his closest friends see privately what he portrays to others publicly? This question must be answered "yes" in all areas of his life: work, home, church or play, or his answer is actually "no." If the people he works with, has class with, plays golf with or plays basketball or video games with, see a different guy than his wife, girlfriend, family or his church sees, then he is a deceiver and lacking integrity.

The life of Joseph is found in the book of Genesis. He was such a great example of a man of integrity—a man resolved to surrender his thoughts and behavior to the obedience of God's commands on his life, whether anyone else saw them or not. His allegiance was to God and not to people. He was not a man who thought if he could get away with it then it was okay. Joseph was just straight up honorable and righteous.

If a guy's integrity has been lost or damaged, be encouraged; it can be restored through time with the power of God at work in his life. God did that restoration work in the lives of King David and Samson. Clearly, these men suffered great loss because of their lapse in moral integrity, but God, being gracious and merciful, restored them to a right relationship with himself and enabled them to do great things on his behalf.

There are three particular demonstrations of integrity gleaned from the life of Boaz that are good for guys, as well as girls to comprehend. It is with great encouragement that girls should watch for these attributes before entering into an exclusive relationship with a guy. He must be a guy with integrity or she will find herself in a miserable place. The following list are not all of the ways where integrity is demonstrated, but at least some areas to begin with and to consider the status of integrity in a guy's personal life.

1. Boaz demonstrated integrity by being *honest*.

When confronted with the offer from Ruth to be his wife, he was compelled to tell her that there was a relative who was closer in the lineage than he was and therefore had first choice on the inheritance that was due. This closer relative had the first choice in taking Ruth as a wife as well.

It is so amazing that Boaz's integrity trumped his feelings over her choosing him and presenting herself as willing to marry him. Instead of taking advantage of this very desirable gift of marriage to this young woman, he was quick to defer to the other relative so he was keeping the law and the ethics of family inheritance. What a wonderful testimony of a follower of Christ – when a guy's personal desires are sacrificed for the pleasure of God's blessing.

Great respect is earned when a guy's girlfriend, wife or any of his friends sees him make an honest move when no one else would ever know. Boaz knew there was a chance he could lose Ruth to the closer relative, but he trusted God with his future in finding a wife and therefore had no fear in being honest, because he had nothing to lose.

There will come a time when guys and girls will be faced with the conflict of getting something now or trusting God to provide it in an unknown future. There may be a time when the honest choice, the choice of integrity, causes them to lose out, or miss out or even reap some unfortunate consequences. This is when their faithful trust in God compels them to make the honest choice, because it pleases the Lord. That is enough. They are convinced that God is faithful and will help them through all things. If they trust God they can wait on him to do the *best* things, because God always does.

Consider Abraham and Sarah from the book of Genesis. They did not trust God enough to wait for the baby that he promised would be born to them. Waiting was just too painful, and their impatience propelled them into their own schemes and manipulations. Personal integrity would say, "Wait on God to provide just as he said he would." Selfish ambitions and impatience said, "Use whatever means you have to get that baby as quickly as possible." Sarah chose her handmaiden, Hagar, to sleep with Abraham in order to conceive the child they were promised. Looking at this choice it may be easy to ridicule such a foolish decision, but consider the quick-start ways to God's will that many people may have used as well. Hagar and her baby, Ishmael, were evicted from the camp eventually due to Sarah's jealousy and disdain and the eventual birth of her own son, Isaac. It should also be mentioned that the descendants of those two children are still fighting to this day. Wow—what a little integrity and being honest before God might have prevented.

2. The second display of integrity by Boaz was in his willingness to be *accountable*.

In Chapter 4 of Ruth we see Boaz deal with a legal issue of heirship with honor and the desire for accountability. Boaz searched for the man that was the closer relative, the kinsman-redeemer, and therefore eligible to marry Ruth and inherit her land and possessions. When Boaz found him and scheduled a meeting, he called together some men from the community to gather around the negotiation table as witnesses. Boaz knew that the more witnesses there were to their discussions, the greater security and protection.

Accountability is one of the most powerful and helpful ways of securing and maintaining a guy's integrity. It is not only for helping him become victorious over sin issues, but for helping him maintain victory over those areas as well. In other words, accountability is good when he is trying *not* to sin and not to continue in a certain habit or behavior, but it is also good in helping a guy to continue the good things that he *is* doing. A guy who is mature spiritually will let someone come along side him and ask him about his spiritual disciplines: scripture memory, sharing the gospel with others, Bible study, ministry to others, giving financially and missional living. But he will also let someone be entrusted to ask him about his sin struggles; "Are you stealing from your work place?", "Are you cheating at school?", "Are you maintaining purity with your girlfriend?", "Did you view any pornographic material this week?", "Have you asked forgiveness from the person you offended?"

It is not only good for a guy to have others who are his spiritual mentors ask him the hard questions, but some new questions to have someone ask after learning these disciplines might be: "Are you showing her *favor*?", "How have you shown her favor?", "What have you *provided* for her this week?", "Did you *protect* her body, spirit or character from any who might bring her harm in those areas?", "What actions did you take to protect her?", "List for me three ways you have *affirmed* her by encouraging her and contributing to her strength of character and her walk of faith." What a powerful and profound act of integrity it is to be accountable!

3. The third act of integrity is Boaz's choice of *purity*.

Merriam Webster defines purity as a lack of dirty or harmful substances, as well as, a lack of guilt or evil thoughts. I find the wording so crucial in chapter 4 of Ruth regarding Boaz's relationship with Ruth. The scripture says he married Ruth, *then* he slept with her, and the Lord gave them a son. Note that God does indeed have an order by which couples should live their lives regarding sexual intimacy. This text seems to say that Boaz and Ruth stayed with that order. If guys and girls want to engage in a sexual activity, they should be married first in order to maintain spiritual integrity.

Challenges to integrity regarding purity start way back at creation. Clearly from reading the Mosaic Law, the same perversions of God's design seen today were going on in that day as well. Scripture is clear that sexual activity is reserved for guys and girls after they are married to each other. All sexual activity outside of that relationship is impure and therefore sinful. God's command to everyone is

> "Finally brethren, whatever is true, whatever is honorable, whatever is right, whatever is pure, whatever is lovely, whatever is of good repute, if there is any excellence and if anything worthy of praise, dwell on these things."
>
> (Philippians 4:8 NASB)

God tells us we should get rid of the things that cause impurity. "Therefore consider the members of your earthly body as dead to immorality, impurity, passion, evil desire, and greed, which amounts to idolatry. (Colossians 3:5 NASB)

There is just no room for compromise in the area of purity. Anything that robs the mind or a life of its cleanness or clarity, especially in relationships, should be cast aside. God's word teaches how to be free of these sins.

> Therefore, since we are surrounded by such a great cloud of witnesses, let us throw off everything that hinders and the sin that so easily entangles. And let us run with perseverance the race marked out for us, fixing our eyes on Jesus, the pioneer and perfecter of our faith.
>
> Hebrews 12:1–2a (NIV)

Guys, you must earn the respect you want. Authentic, unshakeable and enduring respect comes to a guy whose life exemplifies integrity. Respect can be demanded in some environments, but what a cheap respect when it is a forced and demanded respect.

God's character enables a guy to have integrity. The Apostle Paul speaks of a hope everyone can have when he says "For I am confident of this very thing, that He who began a good work in you will perfect it until the day of Christ Jesus." (Philippians 4:6 NASB)

Job was a man who loved God and worshipped him always, yet was tested in life like no other. He lost his children, his crops, his animals, and his health. His wife and some of his close friends tried to quench his spirit and say that it was his fault these tragic things happened. They urged him to just forget about God – even curse him. However, in Job, chapters 1–5, Job was commended for his integrity, and God said Job was blameless, and that there was no one like him! Even his friends finally acknowledged Job's integrity. "Is not your fear of God your confidence, and the integrity of your ways your hope?" (Job 4:6 NASB)

James admonishes everyone to be people of integrity when committing to do something. A person's word should be the seal of assurance. He admonishes everyone in this when he wrote, "Above all, my brothers, do not swear—not by heaven or by earth or by anthing else. Let your "Yes" be yes, and your "no", no, or you will be condemned." (James 5:12 NIV)

The testimony of a guy's integrity is secured when he is the same wherever he is and not just in the presence of those he is trying to fool. 2 Corinthians 5:9 teaches that "Therefore, whether we are at home or away, we make it our aim to be pleasing to Him."

Boaz gives guys three strong areas to evaluate in his life. The goal of personal integrity in *honesty*, *accountability* and *purity* is noble. God's word certainly speaks to and encourages each of these attributes of integrity. What about the other areas of his life? The trust he earns from a girl generates an abiding, adoring kind of love in their relationship. When she trusts him, he has earned a most valuable gift. The guy she needs to wait to marry is a guy full of integrity that she can trust. Be that guy.

Redeemed

The term used in the book of Ruth for the next of kin who would be given first rights to buy her property and also inherit her as his wife after the death of her husband was a "kinsman-redeemer". He is called this because not only did he have to be related to her – thus a kinsman – but he was responsible to see that any of her family members in trouble would be helped, vindicated or restored – thus her redeemer. Because the nearest of kin did not "redeem" Ruth and the possessions left by her deceased husband, Boaz became Ruth's "kinsman-redeemer". He would be the one that restored her status in the community when he made her his wife. This redemption was crucial to the family.

> Then the women said to Naomi, "Blessed be the Lord,
> who has not left you this day without a redeemer, and
> may his name be renowned in Israel!
>
> Ruth 4:14 (NASB)

Naomi and Ruth found themselves in a desperate place when they moved back to Judah as widows. All that they owned and even their own status as contributing members of the community were in jeopardy of being lost to the government. But God sent them this wonderful, kind "kinsman redeemer" in Boaz. He loved Ruth. Because he loved her and wanted her for his wife, he was able to redeem her. His agreement to take possession of all she owned and take her as his wife brought new hope, new joy and a new future.

For the guy that has found himself at the end of this book feeling unfit or discouraged at his poor application of these five things, be encouraged by this great news. You, too, have a Redeemer! God's word says that no one can measure up to the example that Jesus set in himself. Everyone is born with a nature that will choose his own interests and selfish desires every time. People were spiritually lost, destined to fail until God sent a Redeemer, the one who would buy back and restore value to all people through his shed blood on the cross at Calvary. Because of his great sacrifice, everyone has been given a hope and a promise that you can be more than conquerors over the hurdles and complications that this temporary world presents. The whole world *needed* a

Redeemer. Families, marriages and all relationships need to be redeemed. Put your trust in God right now by confessing that Jesus Christ is Lord and surrendering your life to follow and obey him. Tell him now.

Guys will need to understand that, in order for these disciplines to be fully developed, fluid, rich and maximized in their effectiveness, they must know the designer and sustainer of all life and health and strength. That Designer and Sustainer is sovereign God.

If you have considered building that tower, that wonderful tower of a committed relationship, counted the cost of making that kind of commitment, and believe you have the resources to complete it, then you must know that the only way you can *know* God is through his son, Jesus Christ. You must follow Christ and surrender all of your own plans to the Heavenly Father who has a plan for you.

God's power and precepts enable you to live out this lifelong commitment. Knowing him is crucial in your development as a great boyfriend and, one day, a great husband. Everything worth anything involves a relationship.

For a girl who is considering dating someone or wants to get married one day, she needs to wait on these five things before making any kind of commitment or devotion. These disciplines are not formed from a survey or based on the opinions of others; they are straight from the word of God and they are timeless. Find a guy who lives these things out, or at the very least is working on incorporating them into his life.

When a guy begins building this wonderful *relationship* tower and considers the divinely appointed role as the leader, should the relationship evolve into a marriage, it will require tremendous discipline. If he goes into it with selfish motives and a survey-based agenda, he will only last as long as the cultural trends and that popular voice will allow.

However, if he wants to go the distance in completing the tower with all of its unexpected interruptions, extra expenses and challenges, I urge guys to get acquainted with the one who can enable them to complete that tower. If they will surrender to the requirements written and established by the builder and designer himself, the Holy Spirit will train, correct and equip them in how to lead their future wives in a manner that is pleasing to the Lord and can last for a lifetime.

Every guy should consider being mentored by a man in whom he already sees these disciplines. Find a man of Integrity who is showing Favor, providing Protection, making Provision and speaks Affirmations in his family's life. That life is worth watching. Glean from men of integrity who have earned the respect of their peers and those they love. Watch and learn from the men who live out the character of Christ every day of their lives.

To the guys who are following God and living out the character of Christ and wanting to please him, carry on! It is going to be great when that girl meets you one day and discovers that everything she was hoping, praying, and waiting for proved to be so worth it.

It is crucial that he determine in his heart to live out these disciplines long before he is in a committed relationship. While some guys and girls will learn of these disciplines after they are committed in a relationship, it is best when guys begin to live out these disciplines early in their life. He should practice these disciplines now, in ways that are appropriate for his age and the level of his relationship. These are disciplines that show girls now what his goals are in becoming a faithful, loving husband one day and how he will achieve those goals. She needs to see that he has become well acquainted with the character of God by living out these loving disciplines to the precious friends in his life while that one special girl will be waiting to meet him.

> It is God who is at work within you, both to desire and to accomplish His good pleasure.
>
> Philippians 2:13 (NASB)

> If you address as Father the One who impartially judges according to each one's work, conduct yourselves in fear during the time of your stay on earth; knowing that you were not redeemed with perishable things like silver or gold from your futile way of life inherited from your forefathers, but with precious blood, as of a lamb unblemished and spotless, the blood of Christ.
>
> 1 Peter 1:17-19 (NASB)

I am praying, and I ask everyone who is reading this book to pray with me, that guys and girls all over the world will look to the infallible Word of God for the standards by which they will live. Any other standard of measure will leave them unsatisfied, confused and disillusioned. Enduring, life-long marriages can happen! When you sit down and consider the requirements–yes, the cost for building this tower that must hold for a lifetime—remember, it can be done! A forever marriage will be a reality when obedience to God's plan is its lifeline. Read it, memorize it and live it out loud.

Guys, Favor, Provision, Protection, Affirmation, and Integrity are part of the blueprint you need to be developing in your life. Start now. These five things don't just show up in your life because you get a girlfriend or get married. They come from hard work and paying the price of what it means to lay down your life for her, and knowing that the only way you could ever do that is through the power of God.

Girls, these five things create a profile of the guy you *need* to wait on before marriage. Many hours, days, and sometimes years, have been lost on relationships that cost you joy and peace in your spirit and in your mind. Pray for patience, discernment, and a resolve straight from the heart of God— that you are, indeed, capable of waiting for a guy who does those five things.

FAQ's

I have included a few of the questions that have been asked multiple times over the years that I have taught the principles written about in this book. I trust they will help you in some areas that you may have had questions as well.

Prayer

1. Is it appropriate to pray together when you are still dating? Does it develop a spiritual intimacy that should be reserved for marriage?

   Answer: Prayer will develop an intimacy with *God*. Praying together gets messed up only if it is made to be a part of your "dating package" requirements. Prayer, in its purest form, is like breathing—it is a moment by moment conversation with your Savior. Scripture teaches us to "pray without ceasing" (I Thessalonians 5:17). Jesus prayed everyday, alone (Mark 1:35), with others (Matthew 19:13), and for others (John 17:6-26). So it seems to me that whether you are dating someone or not, you pray together because you pray already.

2. Why do you think we should pray with a boyfriend/ girlfriend? Or is that meant for marriage?

   Answer: Most of this is answered in Question #1. However, I am curious as to where this philosophy of "prayer only being meant for marriage" comes from? There is no Biblical precedent for this being an issue for marriage only. We need to be praying for each other. I think the mistake here is making "praying together" a checked item for dating, like it is a spiritual standard of behavior for a special relationship. You don't have to pray with each other at all—there is no command of scripture for you to pray with your girlfriend, fiancé' or wife, but there *is* a command, and plenty of examples, that you should pray—all the time, anytime, for people, for yourself, in your closet, with a few, with a group, with boldness, with humility and in Jesus's name. This should keep your prayer life vibrant and active, organic and constant.

3. How can I make my prayer life better when praying for my future spouse and the men who are friends in my life? Is there scripture to support specifically what needs prayer?

    Answer: Jesus gave us an example of how we should pray in Matthew 6:5–13. Examine those elements and make them a part of your specific prayer time. You also have been given a huge measure of grace in being able to approach the throne of God to ask and receive in Hebrews 4:14–16.

    Regarding your question "can I ask for a specific thing regarding a wife/husband?"—there is an example of that in a passage of scripture about Abraham's worker that was commissioned to go find a wife for Isaac, Abraham's son. Abraham gave some general directives about who to look for and where etc., but as the worker traveled to the territory he was to look for a woman, he began to ask God for some *very* specific signs regarding his mission. You can read these in Genesis 24:12–14. I am not suggesting that you pray this way, but I am just pointing out that there is a precedent in scripture for making specific requests.

4. What is one way to pray for a woman? How?

    Answer:
    *   Pray the scripture.
    *   Pray she will obey the commands of Christ as a follower of Christ. If she doesn't have a personal

relationship with Jesus Christ, then pray that she will come to know and trust Christ and give her life to Him by faith.

- Pray specifically that she will mature in her spiritual gift(s) from God as found in Ephesians 4:7, 11–12 and 1 Corinthians 12:4–11 and Romans 12:4–8.
- Pray for her to develop the nature & character traits of the virtuous woman in Proverbs 31:10–31

Waiting

Do you not know? Have you not heard? The Everlasting God, the Lord, the Creator of the ends of the earth does not become weary or tired. His understanding is inscrutable. He gives strength to the weary, And to him who lacks might He increases power. Though youths grow weary and tired, And vigorous young men stumble badly, Yet those who wait for the Lord will gain new strength; they will mount up with wings like eagles, they will run and not get tired, they will walk and not become weary.

Isaiah 40:28–31 (NASB)

1. How do you wait for the person God has for you?

Answer: I know what you are asking, but my answer is going to redirect you. The way you wait for the person, is to wait for God. Think of a waiter in a restaurant. Why are they called waiters? Because they are waiting on the needs of whoever they are serving. They come by often to see how they can serve. They also come when they are summoned. Your waiter will replenish, refill, and try to do everything they can to meet your needs. I think this is a beautiful illustration of what we do when we are waiting on God to respond to our petitions and answer the desires of our heart. You *serve* him—that's how you wait. It's not an idle wait; it's an active, hopeful, energetic wait. So my encouragement to you is to focus your waiting on the one who knows everything you need and desire. Be about the Lord's business and obeying his call on your life. That is when waiting gets really fun.

2.   What are some good ways to be patient when waiting?

Answer:
- Drink in all the truths of Gods word. Memorize the principles, stories, and scripture verses that will equip you to live a Godly life. Be ready for any occasion to give a reason for the hope that is in you which is Jesus Christ.
- Study the characteristics of a Godly man or woman that we are given in the Bible. You do not have to wait for marriage to be a man or woman of God. You can and need to be that now.
- Love people—just give your life away. Look for ways to serve in missions or any ministry area where you

see a need, whether in your church, community, or in lands far away.

3. How would I go about waiting on a girl who may not exhibit some of the traits we learn about in the Bible?

    Answer: I am hearing you say you *want* to wait on a girl that exhibits all of the biblical traits and disciplines a wife/woman should have. If this is a correct understanding—I am thankful you are waiting. Refer to my answer in the question about *how* to wait. However, while you are waiting for God, pray for this special woman in your life to learn from older believers and be discipled in her walk with Christ, so that she can mature and be strengthened in these areas of weakness. Remember, no one is going to be perfectly mature in all aspects of their spiritual disciplines. This is what we spend a lifetime developing and changing. But what you need to see is a life lived out in pursuit of these. If she is faithfully keeping her eyes on Jesus and desiring to change the weaker areas by letting them be refined by God's workmanship, then carry on. "Not that I have already obtained it or have already become perfect, but I press on so that I may lay hold of that for which also I was laid hold of by Christ Jesus" (Philippians 3:12, NASB).

4. How can I be sure a man's heart is truly in pursuit of my heart? I want to wait on the man whom God has saved

for me, but how can I be sure I'm not missing out on the right man?

Answer: Your best assurance will come when you observe the fruit of the Spirit listed in Galations 5:22: love, joy, peace, patience, kindness, goodness, faithfulness, gentleness and self-control, in his life. Look for the biblical disciplines gleaned from the life of Boaz in the book of Ruth, which are also found in Jesus. Watch for these and see if they are exercised authentically and continuously. Not just toward you, but you see these graces extended toward all people. But dear friend, marrying someone will *always* involve a measure of faith. Not a blind faith, but a faith that is grounded in the hope that what you see in his life now will be what you see fourteen years from now.

Regarding "the man God has saved for me" and not "missing out on the right man"—there is some conflict built in here. If God has indeed saved someone in particular for you, he is faithful to keep his promises. He would not relinquish his selection for you, and therefore, your fear of missing out on that right one is unfounded.

However, my encouragement to you is to be diligent, prayerful, and watchful for a man that is living out his faith with integrity in which his life speaks to the fact that he is a man after God's heart. At the same time, you need to be developing your faith walk as well. Don't let fear entrap you. Scripture teaches us to "Delight yourself in the LORD and He will give you the desires of your heart." (Psalm 27:4 NASB) This passage is in the middle of a chapter about God's provisions when dealing with an enemy. I think this promise is based on his perfect, unchanging character and is therefore still a promise we can claim as well. So delight in him, and you will find that the desires of your heart will begin to look like the desires of his.

Past Hurts

1. What does a woman who has been hurt by men in the past do, if it's almost impossible for her to trust a man to lead her? Even Godly men can and have failed her.

    Answer: The first response that came to my mind regarding what she should do after being hurt is to forgive. While that may not be the answer she wanted to hear, Jesus says "For if you forgive other people when they sin against you, your heavenly Father will also forgive you." (Matthew 6:14 NIV) It is clearly commanded that we must forgive, if we want to be forgiven. And we so *desperately need* to be forgiven.

    The other thought that comes to my mind is how huge the price we pay for sin. Because of the lack of integrity and demonstration of godliness she has experienced from men who claim to be Christ followers, she feels it is impossible to trust a man to lead her. This now has rooted in her life and has become a sin which entangles her in the web of Satan's lies. It has the potential to throw her off course in the design that God has established for a marriage. The enemy knows that the design of God for marriage is that the husband leads. So the enemy is now tempting her to sin by not wanting to trust him to lead, and thus refusing to let him lead. When Godly men sin, when they have failed to live up to the standard of holiness and integrity that he is called to do, it causes someone to stumble. Jesus has a *very* strong warning to all of us when he taught his disciples that "…It is inevitable that stumbling blocks come, but woe to him through whom they come!" (Luke 17:1, NASB)

Tell her to keep her eyes fixed on Jesus. Learn about his character and the way he teaches you to love and what that looks like. Start with the whole chapter of 1st Corinthians 13. Tell her to pray for healing and rebuke the lies that Satan would have her believe, then walk with confidence in the freedom that the Holy Spirit of God gives. Tell her not to listen to the whispers of the ones that would keep her bound to a hopeless future. Live out your life with purpose and intention to share the good news of Jesus Christ with others. Love people and learn how to be friends with guys in your life. God has and will continue to raise up great men of God who want to be like him, and they want to love people like he does. They want to treat their girlfriends with honor and grace. They want to be faithful husbands and raise families that serve the Lord. *Please,* tell her to wait for one of those men while she continues to serve Jesus.

2. I am incapable of giving a guy my heart because even the most awesome guy I have dated has cheated on me, etc. How will I be able to love someone if God put him into my life, because I am now cold-hearted toward men?

Answer: It is devastating when trust is broken. However, that deep wound that seems like it will never go away is not too complex for an omnipotent God. 2 Corinthians 5:17 tells us he is the restorer of all things. He restores beauty from ashes (Isaiah 61:3); he also totally renews your mind, when you offer him your life as a living sacrifice (Romans 12:2). The cold-hearted feeling you have, as well as the feeling of being incapable of loving again, is not what you are left to be in God's design of things. In Ezekiel 37, we read a story where God takes the prophet Ezekiel to look at a valley of dry bones, which represents the *lost hope* of God's people. God tells Ezekiel that when he speaks the Truth that God has given him to speak to the dry bones, they will be restored to life. Sure enough, when Ezekiel speaks those words to the bones laying there on the dry, parched ground, their skin and muscles begin to be repaired, and they begin to breathe again. In just moments they are all restored to life and health. They did not just have their life and hope restored, but we are told they stood up as a mighty army! This can be you, too, precious friend. As a child of God, you are not destined to stay in the valley with a hopeless spirit, incapable of loving a man with joyful anticipation of a lifetime together in an enduring marriage. Listen to the Truth and walk in it – even if you don't feel it. That is a walk of faith. Walk in the knowledge that God is faithful, and he will always keep His promises. (Please read the answer to question 1 in this category for more truths from God's word regarding your question.)

3. How do you go about speaking about past relationships with your significant other?

    Answer: Very carefully. If there was sin involved in your previous relationship or any kind of emotional wounding, or trauma that you experienced that could have an impact on your behavior in this new relationship, it might be necessary to share. I think the honorable time to share these past issues of your life is while you are still at the friend level. This disclosure, while still friends, enables a measure of grace to the one listening, and then they can determine if these issues of your past are deal breakers for them. They can have time to pray and seek counsel and then determine whether or not to advance the relationship or remain as friends. James says to "confess your sins to one another, and pray for one another so that you may be healed. The effective prayer of a righteous man can accomplish much." (James 5:16, NASB) The bottom line is to listen to the prompting of the Holy Spirit and follow his lead concerning when and how much should be shared. He is always right.

4. Being a Christian who has messed up in regards to purity how do you come back from that?

Answer: You come back from moral failure through the power of Jesus Christ, who has shed his redemptive blood for you. It is Christ alone that enables you to come back from that failure with a heart that is as white as snow. This is what redemption is. *Anything* else that you have done that falls short of God's desire for us is covered under the blood of Jesus that was shed for us on Calvary. God's word reminds us "…without the shedding of blood there is no forgiveness." (Hebrews 9:22, NIV) I hope that you will find more help in the answers already given. I loved answering this question, because it prompts the telling of the good news of the redemption and salvation we have in Christ Jesus. I praise God that I am not bound in the chains of the sins of my past. You don't have to be bound, either. "So if the Son makes you free, you will be free indeed." (John 8:36, NASB)